FINN JONES WAS HERE

SIMON JAMES GREEN

Illustrated by JENNIFER JAMIESON

Published in the UK by Scholastic, 2023
1 London Bridge, London, SE1 9BG
Scholastic Ireland, 89E Lagan Road, Dublin Industrial Estate,
Glasnevin, Dublin, D11 HP5F

Text © Simon James Green, 2023
Illustrations by Jennifer Jamieson © Scholastic, 2023

The right of Simon James Green to be identified
as the author of this work has been asserted by him
under the Copyright, Designs and Patents Act 1988.

ISBN 978 0702 30364 7

A CIP catalogue record for this book is available from the British
Library.

Printed by CPI Group (UK) Ltd, Croydon, CR0 4YY
Paper made from wood grown in sustainable forests and other
controlled sources.

1 3 5 7 9 10 8 6 4 2

This is a work of fiction. Names, characters, places, incidents and
dialogues are products of the author's imagination or are used
fictitiously. Any resemblance to actual people, living or dead, events or
locales is entirely coincidental.

www.scholastic.co.uk

In memory of my dad, John Green.

"Is the dog chasing? Is it a test?"

– Ancient proverb

CHAPTER ONE

Monday, 10.45 a.m.

I almost believed it, Finn.

You almost had me.

I wasn't sure *how* you'd done it, and I wasn't entirely sure *why*, but what I *did* know was that you were going to have a hell of a lot of explaining to do. 'Cause here's the thing, Finn: you may not have fooled me, but based on what I saw today, you've fooled everyone else. And when they realize – when they *know* the truth – well ... *oh boy*... I would not want to be in your shoes ... even if those shoes *are* the coolest kicks money can buy.

No sooner had I arrived, at the exact time and place you'd instructed, your big sister Abi hurried up to me.

"Eric? Why on earth are you dressed as a unicorn?"

"A better question would be, why aren't you?"

I pulled the hood down and blinked in the bright sunlight. You would have said this costume slaps, Finn. It took ages to find a size online that would fit me, but here it was: lavender jumpsuit with rainbow unicorn tail, rainbow glitter boot tops, pink gloves, and, the *pièce de résistance*, the hood with cute ears, eyes and an amazing rainbow horn. Just like you'd asked for. It cost thirty quid, Finn. The things you make me do.

Your big sister was just staring at me. She looked *wrecked*, Finn. Red puffy eyes, and tear tracks down her cheeks. I would have given her a hug, but since you always claim I have a crush on her (when I absolutely do not!) I didn't bother. I didn't want to risk any rumours. Or you taking a secret photo. I know what you're like.

Oh, she was also dressed really formally – all in black. Which was odd, since that wasn't the instruction.

"It isn't fancy dress," she told me. "It's a funeral."

I squinted, trying to work her out. I'd kinda assumed she was in on this, and I was just about to say, "Well, is it, though?" and give her a knowing wink, when I noticed that everyone else gathered outside the church was also dressed in serious, sad clothes, and then my mum appeared at my side – also in her unicorn outfit. It's even harder to find an adult-sized unicorn costume, Finn. Hers had to be shipped express from China. I want you to know that we went all-out on this.

"Hello, Abi," Mum said, approaching your sister. "I'm so sorry for your loss."

Abi nodded.

Then Mum glanced at the crowd over Abi's shoulder and visibly jumped. She hissed through gritted teeth, "Eric? No one else is dressed as a unicorn!"

"That's because it isn't fancy dress," Abi repeated.

"But Eric got the invite," Mum replied. She was trying to keep her tone light, but I could hear the panic in it. You know how Mum likes to be so organized and in control, Finn? Everything done the right way at the right time. Nothing left to chance, right? She's worse than me. Coming to your "funeral" in fancy dress if we weren't meant to would be a nightmare for her. It would be a nightmare for me too, but I think twelve-year-old boys are expected to be a little bit bananas so

I'm not sure it matters as much. "Show Abi the invite, Eric!" Mum insisted.

So I did.

Finn Jones Esquire cordially invites you to his ...

"Oops, I'm dead!" party! Aka funeral.

Dress code: unicorns!
There's bound to be food!
(Hopefully barbecue chicken wings and
maybe some ramen and other stuff!)
Thursday 31st July, 11 a.m. St Peter's Church.

Abi looked up from reading and blew out a breath. "I don't know where this came from, but we didn't send invites out. We just called or messaged family and friends."

"Yes," Mum said. "We got the message. And then we got this."

"Well, it didn't come from us," Abi continued. "I'm guessing that it's some sort of practical joke. From Finn."

I couldn't help but smile, because, fair play, that was a good one. And you got my mum too. Top tier pranking, buddy.

"How could the invite possibly be from Finn?" Mum asked.

"No idea, but this is exactly the sort of trick my little brother would pull…" Her voice cracked and she wiped her eyes with a tissue. "Even now. Even when he's no longer with us."

Mum's eyes were nearly popping out. "But … he got the date right and everything!"

Abi sighed. "Always one step ahead of everyone, right?" She turned to me and gave me a kind of sad smile. "Eric, he told me to give you this."

She handed me a large envelope that had a wax seal on the back.

"I had strict instructions not to open it, just to give it to you on the day of his funeral," she continued. "I wouldn't normally do a single thing that muppet said, but … well." She swallowed. "Don't worry about the costume, it's fine."

"It's a hundred per cent polyester," I said, hoping she'd

be impressed by that at least – especially in this heat.

"Yeah, that's not a selling point, Eric," she said, turning and walking towards the entrance of the church.

"I should have checked!" Mum said aloud to herself, her voice all high-pitched and quivering. "I *would* have checked, but I didn't want to bother Finn's parents with silly questions when they'd just lost their son…"

I grinned at her. "This is *so* Finn."

"I'm going to kill him," Mum muttered.

"He's already dead, Mum," I replied. (I didn't manage tears, Finn, but I did say it with conviction. A pretty good bit of improv, don't you think? Funny too!)

Mum shook her head and followed Abi. And even though this was meant to be a sad day, and even though I should have probably been playing along with whatever nonsense you'd cooked up this time, I found myself smiling. I hope I didn't give the game away, but getting an invite to arrive with the correct time and date of your supposed funeral? When you couldn't have known those things? Well, let's just say the pieces of this jigsaw were starting to slot into place.

I turned the sealed envelope over in my hands. I honestly felt I was about to get some kind of answer that would put an end to all this. Turned out I was wrong about that, huh? That wasn't the end at all. It was just the beginning.

CHAPTER TWO

Inside the first envelope were two further envelopes, one of which had "READ ME FIRST!" scrawled on the front.

Heeeeey, buddy!
   OK, so, if you're reading this, it means ...
well, hopefully it means you're standing
outside the church DRESSED AS A UNICORN
calling me all the bad words that your mum
thinks you don't even know. You're welcome,
Eric! I just couldn't stand the thought of
everyone moping about, being sad, you know?
I think you (and specifically, your costume)

will add a bit of fun to this whole awful thing.

Look, I know things have been rocky with us recently, but I'm dead now, so joke's on you – surprise! And you wouldn't deny a dead kid his final wishes, would you? 'Cause I fancy having some fun. We always used to have fun, right? So how about one last adventure? Think of it like … a treasure hunt. With some pretty valuable treasure at the end of it. Intriguing, huh? But you gotta follow my exact instructions to the letter. These are my dying wishes, so you have to do it. I don't make the rules. Whatever I say, you gotta do. Exactly as I say it. It won't work otherwise. And, trust me, you want this to work. It'll totally be worth it. Never know what (or who) you might find!

It starts now. Here's your first instruction: rip up whatever nonsense you were planning on reading at my funeral. The speech you <u>are</u> going to read out is inside the second envelope. Do not open it until you're at the pulpit! Don't try and wriggle out of any of it, or change the words, or whatever. No admitting that I wrote it either, that would totally spoil the fun. You read it as it's written, buddy, that's all you gotta do.

Easy, right? 😈

Over and out!

Finn X

"Roger that," I murmured to myself.

Huh. You sure were laying it on thick with all that "dead kid" stuff, Finn, but I guess that's all part of your plan.

Meanwhile, that smiling devil emoji could only mean more embarrassment was heading my way, and you *know* how much I hate surprises, Finn! That's why I always get you to tell me what present you've got for my birthday every year – I need to know how to react. I need to prepare.

That's why I did it. I opened the second envelope. I needed to know what was in store before I made a

total fool of myself in front of about a hundred people –
including most of Year 7, the majority of whom thought
I was a huge dweeb anyway.

The paper inside the second envelope was blank.

Except for a few lines at the very top.

Eric. I told you not to open it yet. Follow my
exact instructions, remember? You have fallen
at the first hurdle.

No worries. I knew you'd do this, that's why
I wrote the speech in special UV ink. It'll
only show up once you're in the pulpit, where
I've arranged for a UV light to be installed.
No more disobeying me, you bad, bad boy. 😈

"So devious!" I muttered. "Always have to keep me in
the dark about stuff, don't you?"

"Are you talking to yourself?!" Mum shouted over
from the church doorway.

I shook my head as I caught up to her. "No. To Finn."

Mum stared at me for a few moments, probably
trying to work out if me talking to dead people was in

any way healthy. "Right, well, it's starting, so you need to get in here," she replied eventually, nodding to the vicar as we passed by, who didn't bat an eyelid, like a couple of unicorns were a perfectly normal thing to see going in and out of a church.

Thing is, Finn, it *is* perfectly healthy. Because you're not dead, are you? Maybe I'm one step ahead of you this time. Maybe I've already worked it out. Let me explain.

CHAPTER THREE

"Order in court! People of the jury, in the case of Eric Griffin versus the Astounding Lies of Finn Jones, may I present ... THE EVIDENCE!"

Finn Jones loved to plot and plan. He loved playing tricks. And he was a master at the long game. When his sister was mean to him one time, he didn't seek instant revenge … he just sowed cress seeds on to the rug in her bedroom, sprinkled on some water, and waited.

He once spent an entire term convincing teacher's pet Betty Bradshaw that if you shake your booty at a koala for long enough, it'll eventually shake its booty back – knowing full well that we had a class trip to the zoo scheduled for the end of term and relishing the prospect of Betty humiliating herself at the koala enclosure.

Then there was the talent show where Finn made Mrs Weaver vanish from a huge box. She reappeared, three minutes later, on the roof of the science block. To this day, no one knows how Finn did it – not even me, and I was his "glamorous assistant"!

People of the jury: has Finn Jones just pulled off an even more amazing vanishing trick? Because here are some more facts: I've only ever seen him alive. Has anyone checked that it's actually him in the coffin? Everyone's just taking it for granted he's in there – but what if it's just a few sacks of potatoes?

A few months after Finn got sick, his parents found a doctor in Mexico who was developing some kind of new experimental treatment. Everyone got really excited about it, and people did sponsored walks to help raise the money to send Finn over there. But the doctors here didn't think it was a good idea, and there were delays and problems, and eventually Finn and his parents used the money to give Finn the trip of a lifetime instead.

At least, *that was the story.*

I remember now, on a few occasions, walking in to Finn's room, and he was chatting with his gran. And as soon as they saw I'd come in, they'd stop talking and look sheepish. What was that all about, huh?! Well, what if sweet little granny was in on it? What if she and Finn went to see the doctor in Mexico after all? And what if they made Finn better?

The last time I saw Finn, he said this to me:

"Don't worry, Eric – I've discovered the secret of immortality! I'm gonna be around for a very long time! Everyone is gonna know my name!"

People of the jury, I put it to you that Finn Jones found a way to cheat death, but knowing the authorities didn't want this expensive medical advance to be made public (because then everyone would want it!), Finn was forced underground – faking his own death to avoid detection! I put it to you that, probably with the help of his family, most likely his gran, Finn Jones has gone into hiding, but has left a series of clues so his best friend can find him.

I knew he wouldn't leave me behind like this. Not Finn. We did everything together.

And the biggest clue was in the message Abi gave me at the funeral:

Never know what (or who) you might find!

Well, I think I do know.

I'm going to find the truth.

And I'm going to find *you*, Finn Jones.

CHAPTER FOUR

Monday, 11 a.m.

I was sitting at the back of the church next to Mum. The vicar was talking at the front, but I totally couldn't focus. That would be the TERROR I was feeling, Finn! I was so anxious about the speech that the paper was getting damp from all the stress-sweat on my hands. Or maybe I was just overheating in my polyester unicorn outfit. Polyester isn't a very breathable fabric, did you know that? It traps the heat. What a ridiculous thing to do, Finn! Make me wear a polyester costume in the height of summer and trick me into giving a mystery speech to a huge crowd, when you're well aware I don't like the unknown! What are you trying to do to me?

Facts: I had rehearsed my original speech for a whole

week. I had been through it with Mum, and marked every pause, and where to take a breath. It had been typed perfectly on to several sheets of paper in a nice big font that would be easy to read. Nothing could go wrong.

And now, thanks to you, Finn, *everything* could go wrong. And probably would.

I realized I hadn't taken a breath for ages, so tried to gulp down some air.

My chest was so tight.

And my hands were shaking.

Did I need a wee?

How would I even do that in this unicorn costume?

"You're up!" Mum whispered, nudging me. "Remember to breathe, don't rush, and look up from the paper from time to time." She squeezed my arm. "I'm proud of you, and Finn would be too. You can do this."

"Sure," I said, because there was no point telling her I wasn't doing that speech any more, or that far from being "proud" of me you were most likely wetting yourself laughing somewhere. Whatever was about to happen, I'd just have to face the music afterwards. Finding you was more important, and finding you meant doing exactly what you told me to do.

I staggered to my feet, legs like jelly, and wobbled into the aisle.

I froze as everyone turned to look at me.

All eyes.

On me.

I put a foot forward. Then another. Each time the sound echoed really loudly around the church. Why were my trainers so loud? I'd never noticed they were loud before. I tried to swallow, but my mouth was so dry it hurt.

Where were you, Finn?

I shuffled past the rows of people who were all here to be sad about you supposedly dying. Cooper Feldman was sitting in a row by himself, with his mum; he was so unpopular no one would even sit next to him at your funeral, Finn. Like, not even tragedy can upend the social hierarchy. God, school is brutal. He looked at me and nodded as I walked by. I nodded back. I felt sorry for him. All your football mates were there. Even

Ethan Matthews – football captain, prefect, straight-A student and Year 7 heartthrob (yeah, he sure got all the *good* genes!) – was there, with his styled blonde hair and his tailored suit. Congratulations, Finn. Your pretend funeral even attracted the cool kids.

No one seemed to react to the fact I was randomly dressed as a very sweaty unicorn until a small girl in the front row (I guess she was some kind of cousin?) shouted, "WHY IS THAT BOY RANDOMLY DRESSED AS A VERY SWEATY UNICORN?" and everyone laughed.

Not the start I was hoping for, but whatever amuses you, Finn.

I walked up the three steps to the pulpit, looked out at the crowd and swallowed the massive lump in my throat. Finn, I want it on record that you've gone too far this time. Your poor parents were *sobbing*. Your sister was *sobbing*. Even your gran, who I suspect has helped you with this whole thing, was *sobbing*. I mean, is she in on this, or not? Or is she just a really good actor? Either way, you've caused a right mess, my friend, and if you want my prediction: you are going to be grounded like you've never been grounded before. Maybe for the rest of your life even, I don't know.

I locked eyes with Mum at the back and she nodded at me, giving me an encouraging smile.

Ugh. I couldn't put it off any longer.

Hands still quivering, I unfolded the clammy paper and held it under the UV light. And, just like you said, the words of the speech magically glowed. I cleared my throat. I would never be ready for this, so I decided I might as well just start.

"There are many things I could tell you about my best friend Finn Jones. I could tell you that he absolutely hated unicorns and made me promise I would never dress up as one for his funeral because it would be really disrespectful…"

There were murmurs of dismay from the audience. They didn't understand your sense of humour, Finn! And, frankly, neither did I.

"I could tell you that he was the smartest kid in our year, and only ever failed tests deliberately, so as not to rub everyone else's noses in all his intelligence…"

People actually nodded at this, even though it wasn't remotely true.

"Funny? Oh boy, was he funny. Finn Jones had the best jokes – he made me laugh every single minute I spent with him. If he wasn't destined to become a brain surgeon, astronaut or some kind of cool scientist, he would have had a great career as a stand-up comedian. Let me tell you what is probably his best joke…"

I braced myself because, based on the speech so far, this was going to be a cringe fest of epic proportions.

"How many tickles does it take to make a squid laugh? Ten-tickles."

Awful.

Embarrassing.

But, amazingly, everyone laughed! The whole crowd! A couple of people even clapped. I have never, never told a joke before that's been greeted by a proper laugh. And now this! For the worst joke on the planet! I couldn't help it – even though I was still scared about what else was in this speech – I smiled.

"Smart, funny, he was also, in my humble opinion, the most handsome boy in Year 7…" I didn't dare look over at Ethan Matthews, but I was pretty sure he and the popular kids would have something to say about that claim. "Finn had seriously good bone structure. Great hair. His eyes – they were mesmerizing; his smile – enchanting; the other bits of him – like his feet and arms and stuff – were also pretty cool. He was strong, he was fast, he was agile, coordinated, like an Olympic gymnast; he baked delicious cupcakes, which actually had moist sponge and didn't just rely on a whole load of icing to make them tasty; he had the voice of an angel and sang 'The Edge of Glory' better than Lady Gaga; kept his room tidy, never left wet towels strewn all over the bathroom, or his boxers on the floor..." (You need to know your sister was shaking her head at this like it was lies, Finn.) "He had great aim when having a pee." (Your mum actually snorted at this line, Finn!) "He could use chopsticks, he recycled, he was kind to old people and dogs, ate vegetables without being forced, was polite and courteous, knew no swear words whatsoever" – (I mean, that's definitely not true, Finn!) – "saved rainforests, single-handedly cut worldwide carbon emissions, brokered peace deals between warring nations..."

I locked eyes with my mum again. If you asked me to

describe her expression, I would say it was somewhere between horror and disgust.

But I was on a roll now, so I just carried on: "He launched a multi-million-pound fashion brand, fought an alien invasion, discovered penicillin, invented the television, invented an extraordinary flying machine, which later became known as an aeroplane, and transformed travel" – (What was this rubbish?!) – "solved world poverty, owned a really big mansion on a private island, owned New Zealand and a few other really cool countries, remained unbeaten champion at Hungry Hippos for five years straight, and was most epic at the dance move known as flossing. Actually, that's a bit of an exaggeration..."

Thank goodness he was admitting this was all a joke...

"... Finn wasn't the most epic at flossing ... BECAUSE I AM!"

Oh no!

Everyone was staring at me. Some of them just looked confused. Some of them looked like they were pitying me. I think my mum was probably about to speed dial the counsellor she's been on about me talking to ever since you "died", Finn.

It was going to be OK, because my plan was just to ignore the stuff about flossing and carry on reading. Until...

"Go on then!"

It was the mouthy girl at the front. The one who'd asked why I was dressed as a unicorn. What was *her* problem?

"No, it's OK," I replied. "A funeral really isn't the time for dancing. I'm just going to carry on reading and being respectful."

I nodded, cleared my throat and read out the next sentence.

"For your amazement and delight, I shall now perform my exceptional ... flossing."

Argh! Thanks, Finn.

The small girl clapped like an enthusiastic seal.

I glanced at the expectant faces of the audience. I knew I had to do it. *Follow my exact instructions, to the letter.* Dammit, Finn!

Honest truth: I don't even know how to floss. In the

end, I just threw in any old random moves.

And what do you know? Even though it was very obviously awful, everyone just nodded and clapped. Because it was a funeral. And apparently you can do anything at a funeral and it's fine.

Maybe this was where I belonged. Maybe I should consider funeral director as a career. It felt like people understood me here.

I stopped dancing and received more polite clapping. There were only a few more lines to go. *You can do this, Eric*, I told myself.

"But more than all these amazing things which really mean Finn should be considered for a sainthood – I HOPE YOU'RE LISTENING, MISTER VICAR MAN…"

The vicar nodded.

"… Finn Jones was my friend. We laughed together, we cried together, we faced the horror of SATs together, we were just growing up together, really. And now we're not, and I miss him, and—" My throat suddenly went tight, and I could feel tears pricking behind my eyes, because I … I *do* miss you, Finn, I miss you loads, and there's stuff I need to say to you, stuff I didn't get the chance to explain, and for a second I couldn't carry on, couldn't even speak because it hurt so bad, and then I remembered … DUH! You're not really dead! You're fine! This is all some game to you, the prank to end them all, and I'm gonna get my chance to tell you everything I want to tell you – I just needed to get with the programme and find you!

So I took a breath, and I carried on. "And the world is a less fun, less happy place with a massive Finn-shaped hole in it. Is everyone crying yet? I hope so; I think it's good to send people on a roller coaster of emotion at these things – some laughs, some tears— Oh, you're not reading this bit out loud, are you? That's why I put it in brackets?"

I rolled my eyes at the next line.

Oh, sorry, Eric, I forgot the brackets.

But then it went on…

(But cool, since I have your attention, well done for almost completing the first task.

See? Wasn't so bad, was it? At the graveside there will be a mysterious man dressed in a long black coat, holding a black umbrella regardless of the weather. I want people to think I had dark secrets, Eric. Everyone will wonder: who is he? Anyway – he has your next clue. Which he'll only give you if you finish this speech. So ... you ready? Deep breath, you can do it!)

My eyes drifted to the sentence at the very bottom of the page. That kid. When I found him, I was going to kill him for real.

"Friends and family of Finn Jones, I would like to finish this humble eulogy by us all honouring my best friend in the beautiful, time-honoured tradition of song. So if you could all open your orders of service, and join me in a rendition of ... 'The Edge of Glory' by Lady Gaga. And – great news – I'm starting with a solo."

CHAPTER FIVE

Monday, 12 p.m.

I knew it was bad because Mum was kneeling down at my height in a quiet corner of the graveyard, looking into my eyes. "OK, Eric," she said, really calmly. "We all grieve in different ways, and I know that this is upsetting for you – that's one of the reasons why we planned your speech so carefully – but ... what did you think you were doing up there?"

I shrugged. "Finn ... wanted me to."

She stared at me. "What do you mean?"

I swallowed. I'd almost given it away. I was to follow your exact instructions, and you said not to tell anyone about you writing the speech. And it wasn't clear if you meant after the speech too, like, forever? Normally, I like to plan and know how I'm going to get out of any situation. You know that, Finn. Like how I always have five different excuses lined up in case I suddenly realize I haven't done my homework – including the fake bill from the vet's to back up my claim that the dog ate it. This time though, I had to think quickly. "I mean ... Finn *would* have wanted me to. It's what he would have wanted."

I swallowed again. It was horrible playing along, acting like you're no longer with us, when you are.

"I see," Mum said. "But did you ever stop to think about Finn's poor family, sitting there, having to listen to your little jokes and watch your dancing?"

"But I guess it's good not to have everyone moping around being sad," I replied, parroting your words from your first note.

"Funerals *are* sad, Eric. They're meant to be sad. You can't joke this away; you have to come to terms with what's happened." She sighed and looked at me with squinty eyes. "I think we should go and see Dr McBride. You can talk it all through with her."

That's the counsellor I mentioned, Finn. See what

you've caused? And I wouldn't mind, but I already checked, and apparently it isn't possible to have a list of things she'd like to ask me in advance. So I would go to this thing, sit in her office, and she would just ask me a series of questions I hadn't planned the answers to! Honestly, my pulse doubled just thinking about it, and I was just about to launch into my pre-planned speech about how it wouldn't be necessary ... when I caught sight of *him*.

The Man in Black! He was all alone and some distance back from the crowd of mourners around your grave, standing in the bright, sweltering sunshine in a black suit, big black trench coat, a black hat, sunglasses, with his umbrella up.

He definitely looked sinister.

And maybe a bit silly.

I mean, it was baking hot, Finn. The mercury must have been touching forty. My polyester unicorn costume was basically welded to my skin at this point.

"I need to go, Mum," I said, keeping my eyes trained on the Man in Black.

"Where are you going? We're burying him in a minute."

I flicked my eyes back to hers. Stared right into them. Because that's how someone knows you're telling the truth … even though this was going to be a lie. "I'm going to go and … *reflect* on everything you just said. Just for a couple of minutes."

Mum's face softened, so I knew she liked that. That was one of your tricks, Finn – do you remember? You said: "If an adult is ever angry at you, say you're going to *reflect* on what they've just said, and they'll love it and think you're taking it seriously."

"OK. But Eric?" She caught the sleeve of my costume as I was heading off. "Your grandma is visiting on Wednesday."

"Right?"

"*Right*. So ... I need you to be on your best behaviour around her. No stunts like you pulled today. *Please?*"

"No problem, Mum. No stunts. I promise."

She smiled at me. "Go on. Go and reflect."

"Awesome!" I grinned, before trying to look more mournful and adding, "I just need some quiet alone time," which was another one of your lines, Finn. Remember? Whenever you wanted to get out of doing something.

I was desperate to get over to the Man in Black, but I also didn't want to draw attention to our plans, Finn. So I ended up doing that weird power-walk thing we usually do in the school corridor when we're trying to get to the front of the lunch queue but know we'll be told off if we actually run.

The man just stared at me as I approached.

His face expressionless.

I don't know where you found this guy, Finn, but he was good.

"Finn sent me," I said.

He just stared.

"I'm Eric," I continued. "I did the speech."

Still, he gave me nothing.

"The speech said to come and find you for my next clue." I swallowed. "So … um … can I have it? Please?"

The man still didn't speak, he just tried to open the black leather briefcase he was carrying in his spare hand, but that proved difficult when he was holding his big umbrella in the other. He tried to balance the briefcase on his knee, but the umbrella then tilted down and smacked him on the head.

"Can I help?" I asked.

He handed me the umbrella, and I sheltered us both from the … lovely warm sunshine while he fished about in his briefcase. Eventually he handed me a leather-bound notebook and a really flashy pen, then snatched the umbrella back.

"What's this?" I asked. "A notebook? But why?"

The man chewed his lip and breathed slowly through his nose while he looked down at me. "Look. Finn gave me very strict instructions about what I should say and how to say it – can you just let me do the talking?"

"Oh! I understand. Strict instructions! That's Finn!"

"He had a plan."

I felt a smile spread across my face and I immediately relaxed a little bit. A plan was something I liked. There was an order, a sequence, a set of pre-determined steps. Yes, I would have preferred it if it had been *my* plan, but following *your* plan was the second-best option. "He does! He has a plan! Exactly! So do you know where he is?"

The man frowned, then glanced over towards the graveside where the coffin was waiting, the word FINN spelled in flowers on top. "I mean ... I've a pretty good idea."

I nodded and tapped my nose. "Oh yeah, sure, sure. He's 'in the coffin', yeah, yeah. But, I mean, where is he really?"

The man blew out a breath. "Look, kid, I'm not a spiritualist or a medium, or whatever; I don't have the answers to life's big questions. Like, I dunno, maybe there's a heaven, maybe there isn't. It's beyond me. I'm just an actor."

My eyes widened. "Ohhhh. Have you been in anything I'd know?"

His face lit up. "I mean, a few things. I had a great

37

part in a BBC drama last year. It was called *Man, In Fragments* – did you see it?"

"No. No, I did not. Were you the 'man'? That's amazing. Sounds like the lead!"

"No, I was a taxi driver." He cleared his throat. "Ten pounds, please."

"Huh?"

"That was my line. 'Ten pounds, please'."

I nodded and tried not to look disappointed. I mean, he's got to start somewhere, right? And it would have drawn too much attention to your plan if you got Tom Cruise to show up at your funeral, never mind how much that would have cost.

"Acting's a really tough game," the man told me. "Full of frustrations. And injustice! Never knowing where the next job will come from…"

"God, that sounds awful!" I said. "I'll cross 'actor' off my list of possible careers then – I could never cope with that level of uncertainty!"

"Still, the magic of the stage!" the man said wistfully.

"Still, the insecurity!" I replied.

"So … enchanting!"

"So ... *the notebook*," I said, quite firmly, because I honestly needed to get on with your plan, and I had a hunch this guy would chat all day about his unstable life choices.

The man nodded gravely. "You must document your adventures in it. You're to write down everything that has happened to you from the moment you arrived at the church today, and everything that happens next."

Jeez, Finn – you're setting me homework now?!

Anyway, I nodded. "Why do I have to document everything?"

"I don't know 'why', I just know those were Finn's exact instructions. It's very important you do this. That's what he said."

"OK." If that was what I had to do, that was what I had to do.

He handed me a sheet of yellowing paper, burnt at the edges. "This is a treasure map."

I grinned. "Stained with tea and burned with a match, if I'm not mistaken!" You and I spent a summer making maps like this once, Finn, do you remember? It was great fun until you accidentally set fire to your shed and destroyed nine hundred pounds' worth of rattan garden furniture. "Wait – this looks familiar. Is this … is this a map of my front garden?"

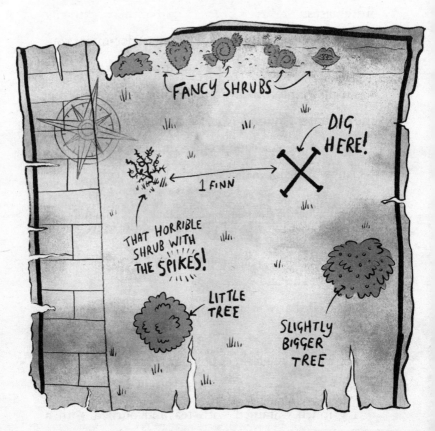

"I believe it is," the man replied. "X marks the spot where you must dig."

"Dig? Dig for what?"

"I don't know."

"I can't dig! That's my mum's lawn! Her pride and joy! Every blade is trimmed to exactly twenty-five millimetres. She even hoovers it; that's how extra she is about it!"

The man shrugged.

Argh, Finn! You sure are having a good laugh at my expense! How am I supposed to dig up my mum's lawn?! You know all about the *literal* turf wars between my mum and the next-door neighbours! If I mess up her lawn, she's gonna think Mr Parker did it in revenge for the time that goat showed up in his garden and he blamed Mum. And then it'll be Armageddon!

"You must do it tonight. Go now," the man told me. "I have given you everything, and I'm only paid to be here another half hour. Tell no one what I have said or who I am. Finn requests you keep this top secret."

I mimed zipping my mouth shut, then quickly unzipped it again.

"I hope you get your big break," I said. "And, for the record, I think you're pretty good. You were kind of scary to start with, and even when you were friendlier, you still had this air of authority."

"A nuanced performance, you might say?"

I snapped my fingers. "Bingo! Yes! Next stop, Hollywood! I can see why Finn chose you. He knows talent when he sees it! He can spot potential!" I smiled to myself, and I wondered, Finn, I thought: *what was it you ever spotted in me? What did I ever do to make someone as brilliant as you want to be mates with someone as ordinary as me?* Maybe I'll finally ask you when I see you again. I nodded at the Man. "Honestly, Finn's the best."

The man smiled. "Good luck, then."

I smiled back. "Failure is not an option!"

I tried to look casual as I sauntered back to where everyone else was standing, but I clearly failed as Mum was right on me.

"Who was that *strange man* you were talking to?"

I knew I wouldn't get away with this. Mum's had a "Stranger Danger!" poster up on the fridge since forever. She once even tested my resolve by getting a friend of hers, who I'd never met, to pull up in her car and ask if I wanted to see some puppies.

I did not pass the test, Finn.

And I wouldn't pass this one. Mum doesn't let anything get past her.

So I shook my head and tried to look *grave*. "I dunno, Mum. But I think … I think Finn might have had dark secrets."

Mum's eyebrows shot up. "What do you mean?"

"You ever hear about the secret service recruiting child spies?"

"Eric. That's ridiculous! Of course they don't—"

Luckily, the vicar interrupted at this point. "OK, everyone, do you want to gather round?"

Yeah, it was time to put you in the ground, or, at least, put your coffin in the ground, so Mum got distracted by that and left me alone.

Wow, Finn. Everyone was crying. Even Ethan Matthews. I really felt like I wanted to cry too – I could feel the tears behind my eyes again, my throat all tight again – but I guess I only felt like that because of how everyone else was being. But then they didn't know the truth, did they? And I did. So there was no need for me to cry. All I had to do was stand there and look forward to the day when I solved your treasure hunt and saw you again.

Thinking about that made me happy. Maybe happy isn't the right word … *impatient*. I just really, really wanted to get out of there. I didn't want to see any of this stuff.

Your mum threw a white rose on top of the coffin. Ethan dropped a football in, which the whole team had signed. And me, well, I almost dropped my note in.

Oh, you don't know about the note, Finn. I wrote it after … well, I think you know what it was after. And I was going to give it to you when we last met up, but you didn't seem to be feeling so good, so I reckoned it could wait. But do you know what? I've decided to let you read it when I finally see you again. Or maybe I'll just read it to you. I planned it so carefully. Every word is specially chosen. 'Cause I mean it.

Afterwards, everyone got invited to the scout hut, and there was food.

Finn – there was so much *food*.

Like, all your favourites.

There was a huge pile of barbecue chicken wings! Honestly, you would have lost it. I piled my plate high with them, but do you know, despite them being perfectly cooked, and despite the glaze being sweet and sticky, I couldn't finish a single one? Not like that time we polished off six whole boxes at my sleepover! And then we had pizza on top of that, didn't we? And ice cream. But, right then, I didn't feel hungry. Maybe I'd just had a big breakfast, huh? How else do you explain it?

Your gran came up to me, and I regarded her suspiciously. Surely she was your co-conspirator, so was another message coming my way?

She's very glam, your gran, isn't she? She was dressed in this very elegant black two-piece suit, with a tiny hat that had feathers sticking out of it. Her eyes sparkle like yours do, Finn.

She complimented me on my solo of "The Edge of Glory" – which was nice, because everyone else had been very notable by their complete silence. "And who knew the vicar had such a fabulous falsetto?!" she added.

"It's true," I said. "He was surprisingly good."

Then she told me my costume looked "amaze-balls", and I am prepared to overlook her cringe attempts to speak like a kid, because she made me laugh by

45

recounting the time you pranked your mum by telling her you needed some tartan paint for a school project, and she checked five DIY stores before someone told her what you'd done. You never told me about that one, Finn, and it made me wonder about other things you hadn't told me … like what all those secret chats with your gran were really about.

So I asked her. Put her on the spot.

And she looked me in the eyes and said: "I've no idea what you mean!"

Not being rude, Finn, but your gran is a bad liar. She was kind of … smirking.

Oh, she knows something, all right.

She's up to her neck in whatever you've cooked up.

And I'm kind of happy that I know that. 'Cause it means I'm on the right track. That I'm not imagining things. Somehow, I felt hungry after chatting to your gran, so we ate some doughnuts before it was time to go.

And maybe I managed a few chicken wings too.

And a little bowl of the ramen.

★

Now I'm home, lying on my bed, stuffed full of food, waiting for Mum to fall asleep so I can go and dig up the lawn. I've looked up online how to dig a hole in a lawn so you can put it back neatly. I've made notes. I'm going to give it until midnight, then creep downstairs. If she's awake, she'll hear me get up, and then I'll just say I'm getting a glass of water. If not, it's game on.

I think that's it, that's the plan. And that's everything up to date in this notebook, just like you asked me. Drew some pictures, told it like it was.

How am I doing, Finn?

CHAPTER SIX

Tuesday, midnight

The first thing I will say about all this is that you did not make it easy, Finn, and you did not think any of this through.

I got out of the house totally fine – Mum was purring like a cat in her sleep – and I went to collect the tools I needed from the shed. According to my extensive internet research, I would require, as a bare minimum:

Tile spade
Shovel
Digging bar
Clamshell digger
Drive stakes

String

A reciprocating saw to remove roots

I had no idea if Mum would have all this in the shed, but she likes to be as prepared as I do, so I reckoned she might. Except, of course, the shed was padlocked because Mum is also prepared for burglars.

So, Finn, I emerged into my front garden in my tiger onesie (the one you got me for Christmas last year!) armed with only a knife, fork and dessert spoon, because those were the only tools I could find in the kitchen and compromises had to be made.

The second thing I will say is that being awake past midnight is not as I expected. I honestly thought I would be totally alone on our street with maybe a solitary owl hooting in the distance. It turns out all sorts of people are up at midnight, and they love nothing more than interrupting a twelve-year-old boy's covert operations.

Most of the lawn was illuminated by the street lamp, and I was able to locate the "horrible shrub with the spikes" easily – I mean (a) it's obvious, the spikes are massive, and (b) we've both spiked our arses on it on so many occasions that the location of that ghastly shrub is etched into our brains (and our arses) and we both want it dead.

(I know you weed on it one time, Finn. You thought I didn't see. I gotta tell you – it didn't work. The shrub not only lives, it's lusher and spikier than ever!)

Anyway, the unit of measurement from the shrub to the X marked on your map was "one Finn" – which I took to mean one length of you, head to toe, lying flat on the ground. You're a bit taller than me, so I made a guess and was about to dive in and make my first incision into the turf when I heard shrieks and laughter from up the road. It was getting louder, so I threw myself down on the ground, hoping whoever it was wouldn't see me.

More shrieks, more laughter, someone blowing a toy trumpet; it sounded like a riot. Intrigued, I rolled over to the hedge and tentatively poked my head above it.

Oh. My. Gosh.

Writing this down for our later amusement, Finn: one of them was Miss Percival, our primary school teacher from last year! She was wearing a wedding veil and had a sash on saying "Bride to be!" And not only did she seem much more jolly than usual (so jolly she couldn't even walk straight it would seem!), she was carrying a giant, inflatable *thingy*. A *thingy*, Finn! I've no idea why. If you want, I'll draw it for you later. It's pretty hard to forget.

All that fiasco had given me time to think, and I knew I needed to make as little mess as possible. I'd promised Mum "no more stunts", and this was one stunt she would never forgive me for – she couldn't find out. I just needed to dig one hole, nice and clean, get the treasure and put the turf back. There was no margin for error here. For that reason, while I was pretty sure about my guess, I decided I should try to be more accurate. So I lay on my back on the lawn, added an extra five centimetres for your additional height, Finn, and plunged the knife in as a marker. After making a rectangular incision (about 30 cm square) around the turf, I eased the dessert spoon in and started to lever up the entire section. It took ages, Finn, but I eventually managed to prise off a section of lawn. Then there was the small matter of digging down. I say "small matter", but it was actually a nightmare task – how deep would I have to go? And keep in mind I was armed only with a spoon, not a shovel, so this was going to take me *ages*.

One hour later…

Did you get that, Finn? One hour! It was backbreaking work; I was exhausted, spent, a shell of my former self, but when my spoon finally hit that plastic box with a low thud, I didn't care about any of that. I pulled it out, sat down on the lawn, wiped the mud from the box, and prised it open.

Inside was a mobile phone, a charger, a Mars bar and a note.

Evening, Eric! Good work – you found it! Every hero needs a little help on their quest, so I've found you someone. Head to "Contacts" and message the only number in the folder. Do it in the morning, though – he likes his sleep. Keep this phone charged at all times. Now fix the lawn and get to bed. Over and out!

Finn Jones

P.S. – Thought you might like a Mars bar after all that digging.

P.P.S. – Remember the end of Year 6? I'm thinking about it and it's made me smile. We were the talk of the town, Eric! (Or at least the school!)

I have so many questions. Why do I need help? Who else could you possibly trust not to reveal your secret? WHO IS IT?! Why have you *typed* your name really formally underneath the note?

I did my best to sort the lawn out, but I'll be honest, it looks a bit lumpy. I don't know what Mum's going to do when she finds it … or rather, I do know, and I'm planning to buy a one-way ticket to Australia.

I was just stamping down on the turf when it happened.

I suddenly shivered. Like … *eyes were on me.*

I straightened up, the stillness of the night enveloping me.

And then…

Movement. In the bushes.

And then nothing.

And I can't be totally sure, but…

Someone had been watching me.

CHAPTER SEVEN

Tuesday, 2 a.m.

I'm still awake. I can't sleep. I've eaten the Mars bar and I think maybe I'm on a sugar high, but also I'm dying to know whose number is in the phone. It's charging up from empty as I write. You've got a plan, Finn, I know you have, and while I'd still rather it was *my* plan, your plan is better than no plan, and that's why I can deal with it. I've just gotta follow it.

So … I've been thinking about the end of Year 6, since you mentioned it in your note. It makes me happy to think about that. And I wonder if you remember it like I do?

OK, so…

WAVY LINES = FLASHBACK!

It was tradition in our school that you come in fancy dress on the very last day of Year 6, your last day ever at the school. It was a really big deal, and everyone had been planning their outfits for weeks. Some kids' parents had gone all-out, hiring elaborate costumes from swanky shops in London. Ellie Morris had actually got hold of some gear from the West End production of *Frozen*. Half the boys were coming as Spider-Man. And me ... well, thing was, it wasn't just me, was it? It was you as well. We were a pair; we came as a twosome, so we needed an outfit for a duo as iconic as we were!

I did so much research. The others planned for weeks, but I was planning for *months*. I'd shortlisted a few options: R2-D2 and C-3PO, Snoopy and Woodstock, Scooby Doo and Shaggy, Bert and Ernie ...

and eventually settled on Mario and Luigi. The perfect pair! We both loved gaming, and the fact those two were a little bit retro just made the idea even more cool. More than that though, they were brothers. And while we aren't technically brothers, Finn, it has always felt like we are.

You agreed to my plan and I set about organizing everything. I presented Mum with the website of a company down in London that had the costumes and could send them to us. Everything was set up. We were going to look fabulous and the photos would be epic.

And then the day before our last day, Mum got this email saying there'd been a problem with the delivery; it'd been delayed due to an issue at the depot, and the costumes wouldn't arrive until Friday … which would be too late.

I'd planned everything. And now it had all gone wrong.

I lost it, Finn, didn't I? Do you remember how upset I was? Didn't even want to go to school for our final day.

But you calmed me down, and told me not to panic, and said we would still go as a double act.

And I said, "Oh yeah? Like what? Cover ourselves in pasta and cheddar and go as that famous duo *mac and cheese*?!"

"I was thinking Fred Astaire and Ginger Rogers," you replied.

So I had NO IDEA what you were talking about, but it turned out Fred Astaire and Ginger Rogers were movie stars from the olden days, who were famous for their dancing. And one of them was a woman.

You put your hand up. "I volunteer to wear the dress. Unless you want to?"

"Never mind that, we've no costumes; everything I planned is ruined; everyone else will have professional outfits. We're going to be laughed at, and, anyway, I can't dance!" I said.

"Sure you can," you replied. "And we'll find a way to make it work – you'll see."

"But … how will people react? Will they even know who Fred and Ginger were? What if everyone just thinks we're weird?"

You shrugged. "Honestly, Eric? I don't really care. *We'll* know. And we'll have a good time. Who cares what people think?"

Well, *me*, Finn. I cared. I was sure that if we walked in as Mario and Luigi everyone would know who we were, and everyone would think it was brilliant. *Because I'd planned for it to be that way!* Now it was a complete unknown. And I was miserable and terrified.

That evening, you taught me part of a dance routine from a musical comedy called *Top Hat*, which was one of their most famous. Then we raided your gran's wardrobe for your outfit and she took us around town to pick up mine. And the next morning, we walked into school on our final day, me in a top hat and tails, and you in this absolutely ridiculous dress. I got nervous when I saw the looks on the faces of some of the parents, but I think you clocked it too, and rather than let it bother you, you launched into the routine, and I followed, and we tap-danced and you spun me around and everyone laughed and clapped.

No way would I have ever done that on my own.

Somehow, you made me just … go with the flow. And things turned out better than I could have ever planned.

And even though the dress you wore was this tatty old thing from the back of your gran's wardrobe, and even though my top hat was from a joke shop and my suit borrowed from your gran's amateur dramatic society, and everyone else had spent loads on their costumes, we aced it that day; we were the talk of the school. Because it was you and me. We're better together. Everything's better with you. That's why I need you back, Finn.

Was that a really good day for you too?

Whenever I looked at you, you were smiling, so I'm guessing it was.

"Do it big, do it right, and do it with style!" That's what you said, Finn. Well, apparently Fred Astaire said it first, but that's how I always think of you, and I always feel that confidence whenever I'm with you. Go big or go home, right?! I felt like we could take on the world together that day. It felt like nothing would ever stop us.

And I still feel like that.

Invincible. That's what you are, Finn. You shine too brightly, like some kind of fire that rages, and nothing's ever gonna put it out.

Which is how I know you're still here.

You have to be, because I'm nothing without you.

CHAPTER EIGHT

Tuesday, 8.30 a.m.

I woke up smiling because I'd been dreaming about you and, just for a moment, I forgot that you weren't around right now.

Then I caught sight of the mobile phone on my bedside table. It was morning now, so I could message the number, just as you instructed.

> Um ... hello? This is Eric Griffin. Finn told me to message you. Something about a quest you're joining me on? OK, thanks.

I waited. But I didn't have to wait long:

Cool, I'm just on the toilet. Gimme twenty mins.

Was that twenty minutes they needed on the toilet? Had you set me up with a sidekick who had a bad case of explosive diarrhoea, Finn? (No need to answer that; it's exactly the sort of thing you'd find hilarious.)

Also: texting on the toilet? Unsanitary.

Also: too much information!

Anyway, then it all kicked off.

I heard this bloodcurdling scream from the front garden, so I knew Mum had discovered the lawn, and I knew that I probably hadn't put all the turf back as neatly as I needed to.

I rolled out of bed, pulled some joggers on, put on my best "acting surprised and worried" face, trotted downstairs and into the front garden, where Mum was pacing around, red with rage.

"Mum? What's up?" I said.

Mum didn't say anything, she just gestured to the lawn.

I followed her gaze. Honestly, it didn't even look that bad!

I played it cool. "What?"

Mum frowned. "Look at the lawn!" She lowered her voice. "Looks like moles! And it wouldn't surprise me if Mr Parker from next door introduced them into our garden!"

"Aw, Mum, really? I can't even see any problem with the lawn." But there was no point in me talking because she was already on her mobile. And we both know who she was calling, Finn. The Exterminator. The same dude who was round practically every month, Finn, getting rid of supposed rats, mice, ants, fleas and anything else Mum was convinced we were infested with ... although I'm not sure we ever have been.

"I can't live with rodents!" Mum said as she was put on hold. "Who knows what diseases they might bring into the house! What if one bites you and you get an infection?"

I mean, I didn't want that, obviously, but I also knew we didn't have moles, so there was nothing to actually worry about. She did that thing she always does when she's on edge – fiddles with the locket on a chain around her neck, the one with the picture of me in as a little baby – then she made eye contact with me. "Don't forget you've got swimming practice at ten."

"Yeah, about that—"

"It's important to know how not to drown—"

"I know, but—"

"And then tennis at eleven, lunch at twelve and drama club at one. It's Tuesday, so tonight will be—"

"Vegetarian lasagne for dinner."

"And then you can play a video game with mild peril on your Xbox for twenty-five minutes, before cards with me, fifteen minutes reading, then bath and bed."

Well, it's nice to have your day planned out. It's good to know what you're going to be doing. I just had a feeling the plans you'd set up, Finn, were going to send a wrecking ball through all that.

I tried to push my worries aside.

I left Mum chatting to the Exterminator (and loudly proclaiming her suspicions about how this was all the fault of Mr Parker from next door) and went to find something for breakfast. What I really wanted was a big stack of pancakes, slathered in maple syrup, but you know how Mum likes me to have a wide variety of nutrients, so I had to make do with "spelt flakes" from the health food shop. They're gritty and kinda dry and they taste like sadness, but she's said they'll help me grow into a "big strong boy". Funny, isn't it, Finn? How being "big and strong" is seen as the best thing to be, rather than growing into a "kind funny boy", for example? I know you'd agree with me on that.

I was trying to swallow down my last mouthful when the doorbell rang. So, this was it. My fellow adventurer had finally arrived! But who had you sent? Someone from the football team, maybe? A kid from the year above? Or maybe even Aaron Alexander? He used Lynx body spray, and his voice had started breaking, so I reckoned his maturity could be helpful.

Truth was, those were the best options I could think of, and even they didn't fill me with hope. None of them would be like you, Finn. Sure, maybe they could kick a football, or maybe they were clever, or maybe they'd already started puberty, and that's all pretty cool, but none of them have the perfect combination of attributes that you have. None of them have your sense of humour. I just know that none of them will think it's acceptable to have pineapple on pizza. And none of them ... will like me how you like me, Finn.

Sometimes I think you're the only person in the world who really gets me.

To be honest, I didn't even want to answer the door. What was the point?

But the doorbell rang again.

Don't worry, Finn. I pulled myself together. I gave myself a "good talking-to" just like you always tell me. *Finn would have chosen a companion wisely!* I thought to myself. *Finn has a plan, and I just need to follow it!*

So I opened the front door.

And there was Cooper Feldman.

I stared at him.

He stared at me.

"I ... um..." Cooper stuttered. "Just wanna say how sorry I am about Finn. I didn't get to tell you at the funeral."

"Thank you," I said, then peered out at the street behind him, craning my neck to see if anyone who looked like they might be joining me on a quest was

heading my way. But apart from a battered little yellow MINI parked on the road, the street was deserted.

I looked back at Cooper. It was nice that he felt he needed to come and say this, and he wasn't to know that Finn was actually fine, but I didn't really have time for this kind of thing.

He was still staring at me.

"OK, so, I'm kinda busy. I've got someone coming round," I said.

Cooper's eyes widened. "Ohhh! Oh, I'm sorry. OK. No worries. Well, I'll…"

And he scuttled away.

I closed the door. How much longer until my sidekick arrived?

The doorbell rang.

Finally!

I braced myself. Would it be Aaron?

But it was Cooper again.

I crossed my arms.

"Um…" he stuttered. "Sorry, I know you've got someone coming round, but just to … um … check … do you want me to go?"

I blinked at him. What part of this didn't he understand? "I've got someone coming round," I said.

"You've got someone coming round," he replied.

I nodded.

He nodded, opened his mouth, closed it, then turned and went.

I sighed and closed the door.

Cooper's nice enough, but sometimes he can be slow to get the message.

Mum was still busy on her phone trying to negotiate a discount with the Exterminator, seeing as she was such a loyal customer, so I mooched back through to the kitchen. It had been nearly half an hour since I'd messaged my fellow treasure hunter, so where were they? I waited another five, then sent another:

Hey, it's Eric. Where are you?

You want me to come round?

Um ... yes? I thought that was the plan?

70

No, sure, that's OK! I kind of need a wee anyway, and it's a good twenty-minute walk back to my place so can I use your toilet?

Yes, you can use my toilet!

Thanks! Really appreciate it.

OK, no worries. Just GET HERE!

Jeez, what was with this guy and toilets? Five minutes later the doorbell goes, I open it, and there's Cooper Feldman again. And the penny finally dropped.

"OK, it's you." I sighed. "Finn sent you."

Cooper nodded.

Look, Cooper's not a bad kid; in fact, he's a very good kid – homework always in on time, impeccable manners, teachers love him – but he's a bigger dork than I am, and I needed help with this, not extra baggage.

"You could have said."

"You said you had someone coming round," he replied.

"I was expecting it to be Aaron Alexander, maybe?"

Cooper nodded. "Oh yeah, he's cool. Apparently he has a *skin care regime!*"

"I know. He's practically an adult."

Cooper shifted uncomfortably. "Um, can I..." He did a little mime, like he was unzipping his flies. "It's only that when I get nervous or excited, I really have to go."

I'm not totally Machiavellian, but I sensed an opportunity for answers. "How did Finn rope you in to this? How much do you know? Do you know where he is?"

Cooper frowned. "Can I just go and wee first?"

"Oh sure," I said. "You can wee... I'll tell you exactly where the toilet is..."

"Thanks," Cooper gasped.

"Just as soon as you tell me what I want to know! So, *again*, how did Finn rope you in to this?" I leaned towards him. "What do you know, Cooper?"

"Hardly anything!" he bleated. "Finn asked me over to his house shortly after he got back from his trip. He told me he was putting some sort of treasure hunt together for you, and that you'd need some help. He asked me if I'd be up for it."

"And you agreed? Why?"

"Eric … he was dying. Of course I agreed."

I stared at Cooper. You'd tricked him too, Finn! Was I the only one who knew the truth?

"And that is literally all I know!" Cooper wiped some perspiration from his forehead. "Um, I really need—"

"Up the stairs, first on the left."

Cooper bounded up the stairs two at a time towards the bathroom.

I've no idea what you're playing at, Finn. Of all people to help me on this quest, why would you pick Cooper Feldman? Did you have a good reason, or did you just think it would be funny hooking me up with the boy who once submitted an assignment on how computers have changed our lives, entirely in binary code, and owns a "Keep Calm and Do Some Science" T-shirt? Nice work, Finn. And that's sarcasm, in case you can't tell. Wherever you are, I hope you're laughing, because I'm sure as hell not!

CHAPTER NINE

About twenty minutes later, Cooper and I were finishing glasses of juice in the kitchen when the mobile started ringing.

I froze, heart racing and my stomach doing flips.

"Who is it?" Cooper asked.

"I don't know!" I whimpered.

"Are you going to answer it?"

I took a deep breath. This was either going to be the next clue, or it was going to be you, Finn. I really wanted it to be you. I'd have given anything just to hear your voice right then.

Hands shaking, I accepted the call.

But it wasn't you. Well, unless you were doing a very

good impression of a middle-aged woman who owned a hairdressing salon.

"All right, love? Is that Eric, yeah?"

"Speaking."

"All right, love. It's Shelly from Locks Away! Unisex hairdressing salon to the stars!"

In the interests of accuracy, I should point out that Locks Away! was not a hairdressing salon "to the stars" – everyone in town knows the real story: someone who used to be in a soap opera ten years ago went in there to buy some shampoo this one time because the supermarket had run out.

"Finn has made you an appointment for eleven o'clock," Shelly continued. "So see you in thirty minutes, yeah?"

"This is very short notice!" I said. "Plus I have swimming! Followed by tennis! And then drama club!"

"There's a cancellation charge if you don't show," she replied. "Thanks, bye!"

The line went dead.

Aaarrgghhhh! I had plans! My day was planned! But also ... I had no choice. This didn't seem like a clue, as such, but it was something you had set up for me to do, Finn, and I guess you have your reasons for that.

Getting past Mum would require more lying – er, let's call it *improvisation* – though. And yes, Finn, I know I've been going to drama club since the start of Year 7 because Mum thinks I need to "boost my confidence", but let me tell you: I'm terrible at it! We keep having to do exercises where we have to make stuff up – on the spot! And then the tutor will randomly shout out new twists we have to include. Most times I just end up standing in terrified silence. Once, I cried. (Then had to pretend it was on purpose.) What a mess.

I emerged into the lounge with my swimming kit in a bag. That was a prop, Finn. To make the lie – I mean, *improvisation* – more believable.

"Heeeey, Mum," I cooed. "So, Cooper is here, and we thought we might head off to swimming together, so no need to drive me, OK, thanks, bye."

"Hold your horses, Eric Griffin!" Mum barked. "Let me drive you both. It's safer."

"It's a nice day, though!"

"Yes, for a kidnapping!" She started playing with her locket again.

"Mum, honestly, it's a five-minute walk, it's broad daylight; you have to wait in for the Exterminator anyway, I expect, and I'll have Cooper with me." I stared her right in the eyes to show what I was about to say was definitely the truth and not a massive porky. "Cooper has a black belt in karate."

Cooper nodded. "I can break a brick with a single chop of my hand!"

"Oh my god, can you really?" I said, well impressed.

He nodded again, eyes wide, mouth clamped tightly shut.

"Can you do it now?" I asked.

Cooper turned to me. "We've ... someplace important to be?"

"Oh yeah. OK, Mum? So we're off. Cooper will chop up any kidnappers—"

Mum fixed me with a stare. "And—"

"And I'll text you when I'm safely there!" I said, knowing exactly what she was going to say, because, as you know, Finn, my mother is completely predictable.

And I'm not complaining about that, because predictable is good, and right then I wished life could be a bit more predictable.

On our way out, I noticed an envelope had been posted through the door, addressed to me. There was no stamp on it, so someone must have hand delivered it.

Ask for your usual
at Locks Away!

My "usual"? Well, that would be easy. My "usual" is just a simple trim. Classic and understated.

"That's so cool," I said to Cooper as we walked towards the salon. "About being able to chop a brick in half."

"That was a lie, Eric," he replied.

I stopped. "What? You just made that up on the spot? Even though you didn't know that I was going to mention karate? Cooper, you should join my drama club – they would love you."

Cooper blew out a breath. "I hate making a spectacle of myself. Just want a quiet life, you know?"

I nodded. "Yeah, I get it."

I have to admit, Finn, the way that all played out with my mum, with me and Cooper working as a sort of team to get out of the house? It felt a bit like something you and me would do.

Anyway, Cooper and I arrived at the salon, which was really busy, with a few people waiting, several old women under the dryers that go over your whole head, and other folk getting shampoos and whatnot. Cooper settled down in one of the chairs in the waiting area with a copy of *Modern Woman* magazine, and I settled down in one opposite a mirror while Shelly tied a plastic cape around my neck. "What can I do you for?" she asked.

I cleared my throat. "Just my usual, please."

So, normally this would be when the clippers come out, quick buzz around the sides, blend the back, scissor cut on top to neaten it up, job done.

That's my usual.

But that is not what happened.

Instead, Shelly started mixing up various pastes and potions, disappeared through a curtain which led to the back room, then returned with more pots of paste, and before I knew it, she'd plastered my hair with this thick pale-blue substance that looked like glue. Then she put a shower cap on me. "Now we need to wait for half an hour, so Finn arranged for you to have a facial," she explained.

I was too bamboozled to object. Shelly spun me around in the chair, tipped me back, told me to "Relax!" and "Close your eyes!" and then smeared something that smelled of flowers all over my face, topping it off with two slices of cucumber over my eyes.

I was left like that for what felt like ten million years, in total turmoil because there must have been a mistake; things were just happening, things that were not normal, when I became aware of a really *smooooth* voice talking very near me.

"Number two at the back and sides, leave some length on top, but textured, with a bit of a quiff, please."

An icy chill swept through me. I'd know that voice

anywhere, because that was the voice of the coolest kid in our year: football hero, straight-A student Ethan Matthews. Look, I get that you're on the footie team, Finn, and I get that you're mates with Ethan, but I feel like he's never liked me. Why would he? I'm a dweeb, and I'm not ashamed to admit it. If he were sitting next to me ... I would have to talk to him! What would I say?

Luckily, I was kind of disguised – my face plastered in goo and a shower cap on my head. So I was hopeful his haircut would take five minutes, and then he'd be out of there, long before there was any danger of him realizing who was sitting next to him.

So everything was going well. I was listening to the clippers being used on Ethan while he chatted to his hairdresser like they were old friends, when I suddenly heard Shelly's voice directed at me.

"Okey dokey, my love! Let's get this face mask off and then we'll just apply a little toner and moisturizer!"

For some reason, I don't know why, I thought it would help my cause and help me evade detection if I adopted a disguised voice, and so I replied in French.

"Merci beaucoup, Mademoiselle Shelly, ça va? Je m'appelle Monsieur Blanc et j'adore jouer au ping-pong au club des jeunes."

OK, I hadn't been paying full attention in French lessons, but I felt that was probably enough to throw Ethan off the scent. A different name and someone who enjoyed playing ping-pong at the youth club – you couldn't get more different to me if you tried.

"Eric Griffin!" I heard him say.

OK, so I hadn't got away with it. I slowly turned my head and locked eyes with god of Year 7 himself, Ethan Matthews.

"Oh! Heeeeeeey," I said.

"What are you speaking French for?"

"Just fancied it."

"Having a facial?"

"Yeah, just fancied it."

"What haircut are you having?"

"Oh, you know, just my usual!" I chirped.

At this point, Shelly whipped the shower cap off my head, spun me around again, and started rinsing my hair at the sink. Job done, I was put back upright in the chair, spun back around, and came face to face with "my usual" in the mirror.

My hair was BRIGHT PINK.

My mouth was suddenly very dry.

Ethan sniffed. "That's ... bold."

A hysterical laugh escaped from me, all high-pitched and weird. "I tHinK thERE's bEEn sOmE kInD oF MisTAke!"

"This is exactly what was requested," Shelly replied in a matter-of-fact tone, as she began snipping away wildly with her scissors.

"Not by me!" I squealed.

"Then who?" Ethan asked, admiring his own completed perfect hairstyle in the mirror. He glanced at his hairdresser. "That's great. Thanks. I love it."

"Honestly, Ethan, Miss Shelly, there's been a terrible error here. I did not ask for bright pink hair. I'm a short back and sides guy!"

Shelly ignored me as she continued chopping around my head, like someone cutting a hedge.

"Actually, I wanted to speak to you," Ethan said.

"Oh ... god ... really? Why?"

"Finn was our number one striker."

"Uh-huh?"

"No Finn means we're missing a player."

"Yes, I see."

"So we need a replacement."

"And you want me to make some signs for the try-outs?" It's true, I am a bit of a whizz at graphic design on the computer.

Ethan frowned. "No, Eric. Finn said you'd take his place."

I froze. Then laughed. Then nearly wet myself. "No. No, he didn't."

"Yes, he did."

"No, he wouldn't have done that."

"He did do that."

"I'm telling you, I know Finn. He's my best friend; I know him better than anyone, and Finn Jones did not say that."

The phone pinged.

I did say that. Finn x

I stared at the screen. Swallowed. How... HOW? I looked behind me, to the left and right. *Was he here?* Was he behind that curtain that led to the back room? Was he somehow hearing all this? This was getting weird. But also ... kind of exciting.

"Are you OK?" Ethan muttered. "You've gone very pale."

"Yes, I'm OK." I locked eyes with him again. "Finn wanted me to play, did he?"

Ethan nodded and flashed me his perfect straight white teeth.

I took a deep breath. At least I had a heads up about this. I could prepare. I could learn all the rules, maybe even some strategies, and maybe it would be fine? "OK. Sure. Then I guess I'll play."

"Good man. We have a match today at two against Snarestown Snakes. See you there." He shuffled out of his chair.

"Wait! Today? Really? But I have drama club! And I haven't had time to prepare!"

But it was no good, he had gone.

I didn't know the rules, but I did know Snarestown

Snakes. Everyone did. They were legendary... All of their matches ended up with a full-blown riot, at least three hospitalizations, and several people being carted off by the police and thrown in a cell for the night ... and that's usually just the parents who are watching.

You've thrown me right in at the deep end, Finn.

And given me bedhead-style pink hair to boot.

Although, as I caught sight of myself in the mirror, I admit I didn't hate it. For the first time in my life, I kind of looked ... cool. Or, if not "cool" exactly, at least not a massive dork. Different. Unexpected.

I wondered what people would say.

I wondered how the Snarestown Snakes would react?

Like piranhas when a fresh, tender piece of steak is thrown in the sea?

Would they annihilate me?

But maybe…

Do it big, do it right, and do it with style! Right, Finn?

Maybe I just had to own this, like you did dressed as Ginger Rogers in Year 6.

"What do you think?" Shelly asked.

I turned to her and smiled.

"Fabulous!"

CHAPTER TEN

Tuesday, 1.45 p.m.

"NICE HAIR!"

"THANK YOU!"

"YOU LOOK LIKE A MATCH!"

"I KNOW!"

"KIND OF WHITE AND SKINNY WITH A PINK TOP!"

"YEAH, I GOT THAT!"

So that is what I experienced virtually every thirty seconds as I made my way to football with Cooper. Groups of teenagers in the street, a bloke shouting out of a car window, and even an elderly lady on a mobility scooter. I could tell from their tone that every single one of them was being sarcastic, but just like you showed me that time in Year 6, Finn, I owned it. I didn't flinch. I didn't let them make me feel awkward. I tried to like being different. Head up, shoulders back, I kept walking.

"OK, test me again," I told Cooper.

He held up a flashcard. "What's this called?"

"A football. Give me another."

"How about this?"

"That's a *goal*."

"Good. And this?"

"Shin pads. OK, I know all the terminology. I've so got this. As long as you're prepared, you can do anything, right? Now the rules."

Cooper flicked to the book on football rules we'd taken out of the library. "Who's the only player that can use their hands?"

"Easy – the goalie."

"Correct. What happens if the ball crosses the sideline?"

"It's a throw-in."

"That's right. Ultimate aim of the game?"

"Not to die." I turned to him and smiled. "I honestly think I can do this, Cooper."

"You know what would look good on you with that hair?" Cooper said. "Eyeliner."

I gave him side-eye.

"I just think it would help set off the pink and draw people's attention back to your eyes."

"Why exactly are you here, Cooper?"

Cooper shrugged. "I told you! Finn asked me. That's literally all I know. He had a plan."

"You mean *has*. Finn *has* a plan."

Cooper blinked at me. "'Has' is present tense, Eric. And Finn's—"

"I know what you think, Cooper," I said, smiling smugly. "But trust me, there's a lot of stuff you have no idea about. I've worked it out. You'll see."

I could tell Cooper thought I was being weird, but it didn't bother me. He doesn't know you like I know you, Finn. He doesn't know what you're capable of.

I was feeling pretty capable myself as I arrived at the football club, thanks to all my preparation ... until Ethan took one look at me, shook his head and said, "You're dressed all wrong."

"What do you mean?"

"You can't play in trainers – you need boots. And is that a mouthguard?"

"You need a mouthguard! I read it in a book."

"That's probably for *American* football, Eric."

"What about the helmet then?"

Ethan rolled his eyes and took me over to a row of lockers and tapped one of them. "This was Finn's." He took a key out of his pocket and unlocked it. "Yours now."

Ethan sauntered off. It didn't feel right to open your locker, but I guessed I had to obey instructions. Inside, there was a neatly folded football kit on the shelf, along with some boots in exactly my size. I shook out the shirt, which I assumed belonged to you, only to discover it was very much meant for me, because it had "Eric" written on the back. Wow. You really planned this properly, didn't you, Finn?

And then there was your note.

Well done for walking in here. I know it wouldn't have been easy. I have two tips for playing. (1) Don't overthink any of this – it's not chess. (2) You can't plan - you have to adapt to survive! If all else fails, just don't run in the opposite direction to the ball - I know what you're like! You've gotta kick it, Eric. Kick the ball. Hey, if you get scared, think of something nice - like our unofficial pizza and chips parties! It really helps. I thought of those a lot when things weren't going so good. Have fun! Love ya, buddy! Over and out!

is immortal.

"Roger that," I said, through gritted teeth. *Don't overthink? You can't plan?* The only reason I had been feeling remotely OK about this was because I'd done both of those things! But my eyes were drawn back to your note, and those final two words. *Is immortal.* Written in that old typewriter font again. Immortal. That means when someone lives forever. I smiled. I knew what you were telling me, Finn. You were still here. I just had to find you.

So I was feeling pretty buoyant, really positive, and

I even looked OK in my football kit. I headed out to the pitch, where there were quite a few parents watching on the sidelines, along with our mascot – Deborah the Donkey – and the Snarestown Snakes' mascot, which appeared to be a viper. I passed by Cooper, who was there on the sidelines, giving it: "Yeah! Go, Eric, GO! Who's da man?! You da man! Whoop, whoop!"

"Cooper, what are you even saying?"

"I've no idea." He shrugged.

I rolled my eyes, then froze as I caught sight of the Snarestown Snakes, who basically looked something

LIKE THIS...

So I was going to get MURDERED and no one would even care or get prosecuted for it, because it was a game of football, and people get killed in football all the time. Or, if not killed exactly, really badly hurt. Either way, it wasn't looking good for me. And I began to wonder, Finn – is this whole thing actually payback? For what I said to you? Because two wrongs don't make a right, and I—

The game started – all shouting and whistles and aggressive kids charging about. I didn't have any idea what was happening really, when suddenly, out of nowhere, I saw the ball sailing through the air towards me. I'm not a total doofus – I knew it was football and not basketball, but my natural instincts took over and I caught it, so that was apparently a "foul" and the Snakes got a free kick and scored a goal.

So it was one–nil to them and it was only forty-five seconds in.

At the one-minute mark, the football ricocheted off my face and went into our goal, so it was two–nil to the Snakes.

A whole three minutes went by without incident,

before Ethan passed the ball to me, at which point about ten Snarestown Snakes started charging towards me, some of them, I swear, in armoured tanks, so to avoid any conflict I simply passed the ball to one of their team, which they seemed happy about, and they ran with it and scored their third goal.

It was going so badly, and I was so panicked, I took your advice: I thought about our unofficial pizza parties.

Mum always planned our food a week in advance to make sure I had a balanced diet. Most of the time that was OK, but on Wednesdays it was always liver and onions, and, I'm sorry, but I cannot eat internal organs. I'd developed a pretty good technique of chewing bits of liver, then covertly spitting it into my palm and shoving it in my pocket whenever Mum was looking down at her plate – it worked (aside from having pockets full of stinky liver to get rid of), but it always left me hungry. That's where you'd come in though, Finn. Every Wednesday, just after dinner, you'd turn up at my house with a bag stuffed full of books and papers, so we could work on our latest school project. Mum was always delighted about how seriously we took our homework, and she'd leave us to work alone in my bedroom ... which allowed you to open your bag, pull out the takeaway pizza you'd brought, along with a big bag of chips. "Because I love pizza, but I love chips more!" you'd always say, and the pair of us would feast on a ham and pineapple stuffed crust and piles of crispy fries, while we did absolutely zero work.

The chips were always piping hot, and the pizza always a little cold, but pizza is pizza, and it's good at any temperature.

Mmm, those perfect chips...

Mmm, that juicy pineapple...

"ERIIIIICCCC!"

I shook myself back to the present. The Snarestown Snakes were cheering, slapping one another on the back, and one of them was running around the pitch without his shirt on.

They must have scored another goal.

"Why didn't you stop them? Their striker ran right past you!" Ethan said.

"I ... um ... I was miles away," I confessed.

Ethan glared at me. "You're a really bad player."

"I'll reflect on that."

"You do that."

At this point several of the parents of our team started to wander off, shaking their heads, a few other people booed, and even Deborah the Donkey gave up and sat down on the grass.

You know what, Finn? This wasn't my fault. It was yours! Why did you put me in this position? You *know* I can't play football. You never think how your actions will make other people feel sometimes, do you? Just like your poor family at your funeral. Or just like when you got sick and decided, with no regard for how me, or anyone else might feel, to—

Well, anyway. I guess I don't need to bring all that up again right now.

Point is, you crossed another line with this one, Finn. It didn't matter about planning it or not, whatever I did, I got it wrong. There I was, everyone hating me, everyone laughing at me, to the point where even rival players seemed disappointed in me. The two teams had been mortal enemies before, but I guess I have this unique ability to bring people together ... in shared disgust at how useless I am.

The team did their best, but sadly we didn't quite win.

Or, in the words of Ethan Matthews: "It was the most monumental, humiliating and crushing defeat the team has ever faced and it's all your fault, Eric."

Who knew he was such a drama queen?

I hung back until everyone had got changed and left (they seemed pretty angry), and then slunk into the clubhouse with Cooper to grab my stuff and get the hell out of there. There was no obvious next clue, unless it was something to do with the note you left me, and what I really wanted to do was sit down somewhere safe with Cooper (I guess two heads are better than one?) and work out our next move.

We left by the fire exit at the back – I figured that would be best, just in case any of the team were still hanging around at the front and were planning some kind of revenge. We emerged into the car park area at the back, and – it was really weird – my spine suddenly tingled... *Something* wasn't quite right... *Something* was off ... but I couldn't place what...

"Not so fast!"

I froze. It was Ethan. I think he'd been waiting for me.

"I've been waiting for you," he said.

You see? *Something* wasn't quite right, was it?

"Finn said you'd probably try to leave by the fire exit," Ethan continued. "He knew you pretty well, huh?"

"Knows me. He knows me well. Present tense, because he still does," I replied.

I think that confused Ethan because he screwed up his face and squinted at me, like he was trying to work it out. In the end, he blew out a breath and gave up.

"Finn gave me assurances you would be an acceptable replacement."

"Typical Finn!" I said. "He thinks you can just … *do* things, without any thought or planning. I keep telling him – *if you don't plan, chaos ensues.*" I nodded at Ethan. "And here I am – *Chaos* himself."

"You can't be on the team," Ethan replied.

Well, thank god for that, I thought. However, Cooper had obviously misread the situation and my feelings, because he immediately piped up with, "Just give Eric one more chance!"

Ethan raised his eyebrows, like maybe he would.

"No!" I squealed. "Don't! No more chances! I'm a failure. I failed. I let you down, I let the team down, but more importantly, I let myself down. I must never grace a football pitch again."

Ethan nodded. "OK."

"OK."

"Well, you can come to mine now anyway," he said.

"I'm sorry, what? And why?"

"Because that's what we always do after a match."

"No," I said. "It's fine. I'll go home."

Why on earth would I willingly go round to Ethan's house with the rest of the football team? Surely they'd only want to ridicule me (at best) and, at worst, tie me to some kind of cart and parade me through the streets for people to jeer and throw vegetables at.

"No," Ethan told me. "You're coming round. Because, if you don't, do you know what?"

"What?" I said weakly.

"Never mind letting me, the team and yourself down, you'll be letting Finn down."

CHAPTER ELEVEN

Tuesday, 4.30 p.m.

"Wow," Cooper said as we trudged towards Ethan's house like a pair of condemned prisoners. "Either you've got a death wish, or you really liked Finn and will still do whatever he says."

I grimaced. "Stop using the past tense, Cooper. I *like* Finn, not 'liked'."

"Eric, mate—"

"I'm not your mate; we're just stuck together on this adventure."

"OK, *Eric*, Finn's not here any more. Right?"

"Right!" I agreed. "He's not *here*."

"OK," Cooper said.

"But he's *somewhere*."

Cooper sighed. I don't think he gets it, Finn. He doesn't know you like I know you. I still don't understand why you invited Cooper along on this thing. He's a bit of a downer, if I'm honest.

Ethan lived in a big house in the nice part of town. There were two expensive SUVs parked on the gravel driveway and a fountain in the middle of the pristine front lawn. Mum would have been jealous.

Hamza (our goalie) let us in. He was a short kid with spiky black hair, and he gave me a warm smile, which I suspected was just to lure me into the trap, making out like he was friendly so I wouldn't change my mind and scarper. He showed us through to a big lounge where the rest of the lads were sprawled over several huge sofas, some on their phones, a couple gaming on Ethan's TV, and a few of the more hardcore sports boys competing to see who could hold themselves up in a plank the longest.

Is this what you always did after a game, Finn? *Why?!*

Cooper and I just stood there, awkwardly, until Ethan came in with two bottles of Coke tucked under his arm and some glasses. "All right, boys?" he said to me and Cooper. "Grab a seat. Want a drink?"

"Be careful, it might be poisoned," I whispered to Cooper.

Cooper frowned. "Not thirsty, thanks," he told Ethan.

"Me neither," I said.

Ethan shrugged. "Suit yourselves." He poured some Cokes, handed them around, and I watched various boys take long slurps and not die.

"OK, maybe I'll have some Coke, please," I said.

Ethan smiled and poured a glass each for me and Cooper. "Me and the team had a proposal for you, actually," he said. "Sandbrook Stallions need a stallion. Although, as you saw today, it's less of a stallion and more a ... donkey outfit. And you'll need to swap over because it's murder being the back end of it – you're bent over the whole time."

"Hang on," Hamza said. "I thought we already found someone. Who was dressed as the donkey today, then?"

"Your parents, as usual!" Ethan said.

Hamza shook his head. "No, they quit, I told you. I assumed you'd found some new people."

"No, that's why I'm asking Eric and Cooper," Ethan said. He looked back at Hamza. "Your parents have the donkey outfit at home – of course it was them."

"Nah," Hamza replied. "Dad told me someone collected it a few days ago."

"*Who* collected it?" Ethan asked.

Hamza shrugged. "I dunno. I assumed it was whoever was taking over. Dad didn't say, and I didn't ask. Why would it matter?"

Ethan was looking worried; I could see his mind ticking over, and mine was too, Finn. I held my breath as Ethan made everyone stop what they were doing, demanded silence, and asked, "Were anyone's parents in the donkey outfit today?"

Everyone shook their heads, Finn.

No one knew who was dressed up as the donkey today.

So who *was* in it, huh?

Ethan started babbling about how it was most likely a spy from a rival team, dressed up as the donkey, so they could assess the Stallions' form and strategies and report back.

And I just smiled to myself.

You're so cunning, so clever, hiding in plain sight! A classic trick of the trickster. You were right in front of me today, watching me play, probably having a right old laugh about it all, and I had no idea! I was so close to you, I just didn't know.

Oh, that felt good, Finn.

But I also felt sad.

'Cause if I'd known, I would have come over. I wouldn't have given the game away; whatever your plan is, I would still have followed it. It would just have been good to hear your voice. I think it would have helped, that's all.

The boys were all shouting and throwing around accusations about the spy in the camp and where the donkey outfit was now when the doorbell rang.

"Ah!" Ethan said. "That'll be our *special delivery*."

There was something about the way he said "special delivery" that made the hairs on the back of my neck stand on end.

"Wha-what is it?" I muttered.

A smile played on Ethan's lips. "Oh, I think you're

going to like this special delivery, Eric. It's kinda why you're here."

Ethan's eyes were twinkling as he walked out to answer the door.

And then it dawned on me, and I wondered – and dared to hope – but if this was "special" and something I was going to "like" then was it you, Finn, about to walk through the door with Ethan? Was this the moment? This whole thing with the football team was a set-up, right? All engineered so I would be here in Ethan's lounge, with a big crowd watching, so the moment we're reunited and you walk in and you're all "SURPRISE!" is a big celebration, people filming, clapping, cheering, and it's a party, because that's what we'll have when we're back together, Finn, a massive party. I thought it would be; I was bracing myself when I heard the front door close and footsteps walking back towards the lounge, and I was ready to give you the biggest hug ever, and that's why, when Ethan walked back in with a huge stack of pizza boxes and I realized *that* was the surprise, and not you, I burst into tears.

CHAPTER TWELVE

I was really embarrassed that I'd just started bawling my eyes out, and the team were all looking at me weirdly.

"I just ... huh ... really, really ... love pizza," I blubbed.

I mean, that wasn't a total lie, I do love pizza.

I just love you more.

Anyway, Cooper offered me a tissue from the little pack he keeps in his bag, I pulled myself together, and we settled down to feast on the pizza. Finn, I understand now why you liked playing football so much. The after-game pizza was out of this world. Crisp crust and base, juicy tomato sauce, lashings of salami and ham and peppers and caramelized onion, and all smothered in bubbling, gooey cheese.

"I think this one's got your name on it," Ethan said, opening a new pizza box. "Ham and pineapple, you weirdo." Ethan smiled at me. "Finn told me it was a favourite of yours?"

I nodded and took a slice.

Ohhhhh, yeah! That hit the spot. It was exactly like...

And then I realized. It *was* exactly like the pizza you bring round on Wednesdays, because it's the same pizza company. So that must be what you do, Finn, and why the pizza is always a bit cold – you bring it round to me after you have pizza here. I guess you pick up the fresh chips on the way. I felt weird, suddenly realizing that ... like, there's stuff about you I don't know. And I wonder ... *what else don't I know about you?* But, *man*, that pizza. That familiar taste ... even the design on the cardboard pizza box... It suddenly all reminded me of you, so clearly, and my heart sank because you needed to be eating this with me, we always ate this pizza together, and I...

And then, just like at your "funeral", the food suddenly lost its taste and turned to sand in my mouth, and I didn't want to eat any more.

Not like me, hey, Finn?

I hope I'm not coming down with something. Just my luck to get flu in the middle of your biggest prank.

"Finn also told us about the secret pizza parties you used to have at home," Ethan said, wiping tomato sauce from his mouth. "After our training sessions on Wednesdays."

I could have killed you, Finn! You told him! You told the *whole team* by the sounds of it. You shouldn't have done that. It's *our* secret. What if one of them tells Mum? It'll be game over for our secret pizza night then. And it's especially awkward after I refused to tell Cooper. Now I look really petty and spiteful.

But you like doing your own thing, don't you, Finn? Even when that causes problems for other people. But there's no point dragging that up again, since I'm not sure it'll ever make any difference to how you see things.

I sighed and looked down at the floor.

"Finn made us promise we'd always invite you to our team pizza parties," Ethan continued. "Especially on Wednesdays. That's liver and onions day for you, right?"

I looked up and locked eyes with him. But rather than his eyes being full of disdain because he was so cool, and I was so ... *un*cool, they seemed more gentle – smiling, almost.

I smiled at him. Maybe ... just maybe, the football lads weren't so bad after all.

"Do I have to dress up as the donkey, though?" I asked.

Ethan shrugged. "I mean, it would be good if you could. Although we still don't know where the costume is."

I tried to keep my face neutral, 'cause I didn't want to seem ungrateful, but that really wasn't the amazing offer Ethan clearly thought it was. And, sure, the pizza was great, but why would I? Why would I need to? "Look, guys, thank you," I said. "But the thing is, pizza is something I do with Finn."

Ethan frowned. "Yeah, I know, but—"

"Like, on Wednesdays, that's what *we* do, so I can't be here as well..." I gave them a wide smile, but they were all staring at the floor and none of them were looking at me.

Ethan sighed. "Eric, look—"

"Oh, right, I know what you're thinking. Look, I don't want to get into what's really going on, but you'll find out soon enough. Maybe it'll explain about the mascot costume too, but I'm already saying too much. Well, hey, this has been really nice." I stood up. "Thanks. And sorry I lost your match. But thanks for not being too angry at me." I glanced at Cooper. "Coops?"

"Oh, come on! There's loads of pizza left!"

"Coops."

"And I'm pretty sure this came in a meal deal, which means free ice cream?"

"It did," Ethan confirmed.

"Cooper, seriously, we need to go now," I said.

Cooper tore off a final slice and clambered to his feet. "Ahh, man."

"You know where we are if you change your mind!" I heard Ethan shout as we left his house, closing the front door behind us. That was nice of him.

"Why the long face?" I asked Cooper as we walked back to mine.

Cooper shrugged. "I dunno, maybe we finally had

a chance to hang out with the cool kids, and I think we blew it."

"Yeah, hang out *as a donkey*, Cooper. That was the offer. And what did Mrs Prentice tell us in assembly that time?"

"Can we all try to stand closer to the urinals so we don't wee all over the floor?"

"Not that time."

"Was it something about white socks not being within uniform regulations? She's always going on about that and—"

"AIM HIGH!"

"Right!" Cooper said. "Aim high! Unless you're at the urinals—"

"Stop going on about the urinals! The point is, we can do better than being a donkey. We have bigger fish to fry, Cooper! We have Finn to find!"

"Eric, he's d—"

I stopped and turned to him. "I know Finn, OK? I know him well. He's out there. I know he is. He couldn't have engineered all this if he wasn't. It's impossible. Trust me."

Cooper just stared at me.

"Come on," I said.

I'd actually forgotten that my appearance was a little ... unusual, until Mum looked up from inspecting her (once again perfect) lawn and stifled a scream. "Is that hair dye? Did they do a patch test first? Some people have allergic reactions you know!"

I shrugged. "Guess I'm still here. Do you like it?"

She took a deep breath. "I'm sure your gran will."

"You think?" I beamed.

"No, Eric, I was being sarcastic." Mum shook her head. "You're behaving strangely. Is it the shock about Finn? Are you OK?"

I nodded.

"How was swimming, tennis and drama club?"

I moistened my lips. "Great!"

Mum sighed, like she didn't believe me, but also didn't have the energy to deal with me right then. "A package arrived for you. It's in the hall."

I glanced at Cooper. "Bingo! I bet this is the clue we've been waiting for!"

"What's that?" Mum said.

"Just … I wonder what it could be!" I replied brightly.

"It's a typewriter," she replied. "I opened it to make sure it wasn't anything dangerous."

"Wow. How about some privacy, Mum?"

"The last time I allowed you some privacy, Eric, you brought a chocolate-covered seed bar home which would have taken you over your daily sugar allowance if I'd let you eat it. I'm just not sure you've earned that trust back yet."

Cooper and I sat staring at the typewriter in my bedroom. It must have come from you, Finn, because who else would send something so completely random?

The question was – why? And what were we supposed to do now? There were no instructions and no clues.

After a long pause, Cooper said, "OK, so either the typewriter itself is the clue, a further clue is about to turn up that makes sense of it, or we've already had the clue and the instructions, we just don't realize it."

I admit, I didn't entirely like it that Cooper was so … on the ball. I wanted to be the one solving all this, because it felt like all these clues were you talking to me in a weird kind of way. And I liked that. I am missing your voice, Finn.

"Also," Cooper continued, "look at *this*."

He ran his finger along an almost invisible crack in the front portion of the wooden base. "A secret compartment!"

I squinted at the outline of, admittedly, what looked like some kind of drawer. "You can't be sure of that."

Cooper shrugged. "But knowing Finn…"

"He's *my* best friend!"

"Yes, I know that, but—"

"If anyone 'knows' him, it's me. *I* know him. Really well."

Cooper sighed and looked down at the floor. OK, I shouldn't have snapped at him like that, but it annoyed me that Cooper thought of that first, and not me. Secret compartments *are* totally your thing. I know that. It's not like we don't have a lot of history with secret compartments...

YOU GET THIS NOW RIGHT?
IT'S A FLASHBACK!!

It was Saturday morning, the first Saturday of the month, and I couldn't wait for you to knock at my door, Finn. The first Saturday of every month was escape room day, and that meant that any second your folks would drive up and take us to the latest place they'd found. So far we'd done Pharaoh's Curse (themed like a pyramid with secret chambers!), Area 51 (aliens!), Bank Heist (so many locks, and a massive safe to open), Prison

Break (included an actual tunnel to crawl through), and that day it was one called the Book of Secrets.

I loved everything about our escape room trips. In the car we talked strategy. You reminded me that very often the clues we need are staring us in the face. We'd escaped every room so far even though it was only ever the two of us in there (your mum and dad always had a coffee and waited outside), but that was entirely due to how brilliant you were at solving the puzzles. OK, I admit it, Finn, I am dead weight in the escape rooms – I literally add nothing of value to solving the game. But you never seemed to mind, and I certainly didn't because I got to spend the whole hour with you, watching you work it all out.

The Book of Secrets was set up like an old study belonging to a reclusive scientist. The scientist had been kidnapped, but had hidden a book full of, well … secrets that it was important to find before the bad guys did.

It was a brilliant room – there even ended up being a clue hidden on the ceiling fan. When you switched the fan off, the blades slowed down, revealing three numbers that you had to type in to open a small safe.

But there was this one clue we couldn't crack. It was a combination padlock, and we needed a four-digit code to open it. The first set of numbers had a red dot above them, the second a yellow dot, the third a green a dot, and the fourth set a blue dot. Red, yellow, green, blue – it felt like the colours were significant, but neither of us could work out how.

"It'll be staring us in the face, Eric!" you said. "Look for anything that seems slightly out of place in a scientist's study."

So I did. I glanced across everything that was on his desk. A clock … seemed OK … some papers … also pretty normal … a paperweight… And then I saw it. There was a pen pot on the desk. But rather than containing pens, it had coloured pencils in it. The pencils were red, yellow, green and blue.

It hit me. Count up the different coloured pencils! There were three red ones, five yellow ones, one green and six blue. Three, five, one, six – that was the code for the combination lock!

The joy I felt when it clicked open was second only to the joy I felt when you leapt up, hugged me and told me I was "brilliant!".

Maybe, in that one small moment, I *was* brilliant. The fact that you thought that meant the world to me.

You believe in me, Finn, even if no one else does.

FLASHBACK IS ENDING NOW!

"Look," Cooper said, still looking down at the floor, "all I meant was, I know Finn liked escape rooms because I used to be really envious of you and him going off to do them all the time. It always sounded so cool. I like escape rooms too." He flicked his eyes to mine.

"Do you? Right. Well," I said.

"In case you ever wanted to do one with me," Cooper added.

"OK, well, that's something me and Finn normally do."

"Sure," Cooper said.

I glanced at him. I guess he was just trying to be nice to me because I'd temporarily lost my best friend. "But I'll keep it in mind, and maybe, one time, you could … join us."

Cooper smiled.

"Onwards!" I said. I thought back again to the one time I'd had success in an escape room, and your advice. Was there anything weird or out of place? And just like you would advise, I stayed calm and tried to think in a logical way. Slowly, methodically, going back over everything that had happened so far.

BINGO!

Something *was* weird and out of place! Two things, actually – the writing on Finn's notes! I got the pages out, folded them over, and lined them up:

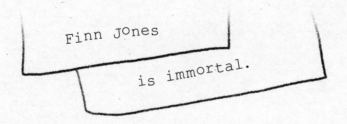

"OK, so...?" Cooper frowned.

"Look at the font," I said. "It looks like old-timey typewriter writing." I patted the typewriter. "Something that this little chap might have produced!"

I watched Cooper's eyes widen in realization. "Type it in. Type in 'Finn Jones is immortal'!"

So I did...

CHAPTER THIRTEEN

Oh boy. Here's how it went down…

I typed in the words and just like Cooper had predicted, a small compartment in the wooden base pinged open. Boom!

Inside was your note, Finn. I'm including it here, because if anything bad happens to me in the next few days, this will be evidence for the police:

Yay! You did it, Eric! I knew you would! You're smarter than you think. All right, now this is where things are going to start to hot up a bit. Are you ready? I hope so. Your next clue is waiting for you ... located in ... wait for it ... wait for it ... (how is your mum's lawn, by the way? Has she fixed it?) ... in a BOX BURIED IN YOUR MUM'S LAWN HAHAHAHAHAHAHAHA! Ohmigod, I am wetting myself just thinking about this. So yeah, it's in the lawn. Sorry, not sorry. This time, it's in a METAL BOX and I've hidden a metal detector at the back of your shed - right behind all the stacked-up boxes and old tins of paint. Just use that and you'll find the box ... nothing could possibly go wrong ... except the shed has a combination lock on it, of course. Don't worry, I've found out the code and hidden it in your mum's Christmas food cupboard. The first digit is in the Pringles. 😈

Over and out!

Your friend, Finn xx

I clenched my jaw. "Roger that, you utter—"

"I need an early night!" Cooper said, quickly excusing himself. And that was it, he went off home to bed, even though it was only seven o'clock. We all know he's just too chicken to break into the Christmas food cupboard, dig up the lawn, and risk facing the wrath of Mum, and honestly, Finn, only you would pick a sidekick who is even less of a rule-breaker than I am.

All I could do was wait for midnight. It was pretty tough, Finn, waiting by myself, with not even your bad jokes for company. After dinner I fancied a bit of gaming – which is usually a good way of wasting a few hours. I set everything up like normal and got our controllers out before I remembered I didn't need your controller because you weren't here right now.

I set it up anyway and left it ready for you, next to your spot on the sofa, because it just felt right.

Wasn't anywhere near as much fun as usual, though. I'd just levelled up, turned to give you a high five … and swatted thin air. Dammit, Finn, you not being here is *not* working for me.

Eventually, it was time to carry out my mission.

Part one: get the code. The Christmas food cupboard was strictly out of bounds because it was where Mum saved all the exciting stuff for the festive season. Over the course of the year, she would add crisps, nuts, chocolates, sweets, jams and chutneys, all kinds of pickles, biscuits … I mean, all the good stuff. I tiptoed across the kitchen, pulled the cupboard door open, and I swear the contents sparkled, Finn! Like some magical Christmas grotto full of wonder and delight. I found the Pringles, gently pulled the plastic lid off, and noticed the foil underneath had already been opened. I peeled it back and found your note.

First digit is 8.
Next digit is in the tub of Celebrations.

P.S. These are open now so you may as well have some. I did! Finn x

Fair point, Finn. And no way would these keep until Christmas now they were open. So I did the only sensible thing and ate a couple. A couple's never enough though, is it? So I finished half the tube.

Go big or go home, right, Finn?

Next, I prised the lid off the tub of Celebrations.

Second digit is 2.

Next digit is in the biscuit selection box.

P.S. Have a chocolate, no one will know. I had a mini Mars bar. (Or two!)

Again, you had a point. It's not like Mum would *count* the individual chocolates. So I had a mini Snickers. And then a Milky Way. And then a Mars bar, Twix, Bounty, the two types of Galaxy and the Malteser one because it made sense to try them all.

After I'd eaten a few more to keep my energy up, I wiped the melted chocolate from around my mouth and slid the cardboard sleeve off the biscuit box.

Third and final digit is 1.

Go on, have a biscuit to celebrate! (I did!)

P.S. Bet you're wondering how on earth
I got this code off your mum? My lips are
sealed ... for now!

"Cheers, buddy!" I said, cramming some kind of chocolate wafer into my mouth. "Just one more? Oh, if you insist!" I continued, stuffing in a Jammy Dodger, two chocolate fingers and a ginger cream.

I put everything back neatly so that Mum would never know (at least, not until Christmas, and hey, maybe I can just claim we had mice again?) and headed to the shed, where the combination lock pinged open easily.

It was weird pulling the metal detector out from its hiding place. Weird to think that you put it there, that some time ago you were standing where I was standing, holding this device, grinning, I've no doubt, at all the trouble you were leaving me to sort out. And for a moment, it felt nice because I felt close to you again. And then it felt sad, because you weren't here right now, and god, Finn, god I want you to be. There are things I need to tell you, to *explain* to you, and not being able to say them is eating me up inside.

Which is why I had to get on with this.

I figured you wouldn't have buried the new box too close to the first one I dug up, so I began my search at the edges of the lawn, thinking I would work inwards. The metal detector made this low humming noise as I swept it over the lawn, and it wasn't too long before it emitted a high-pitched kind of squeal. I'd found the box!

This was going to be a lot easier than the first time.

I dug down and pulled out the box.

Simples!

Opened it…

Wow, Finn. Wow. I don't mean to sound harsh, but I hated you right then.

Eric! Good find … sort of… I may have planted a few trick boxes, just to liven things up a bit – wouldn't be fun if it was too easy, would it?

"Finn Jones is immortal," I muttered to myself as I carried on sweeping the metal detector. "Finn Jones is having a laugh more like! Finn Jones is a—"

SQUEEEEEEEEEEP!

"This had better be it," I said to myself, picking up the spade and digging again.

Eric! Good find ... sort of... I may have planted a few trick boxes, just to liven things up a bit - wouldn't be fun if it was too easy, would it?

Oh my actual heck, Finn! You think this is funny, but you know what my mum is like. I wondered how far you had gone with this prank. Well ... after about ten more minutes there were a series of holes all around the edge of the lawn, the high-pitched squeal of the metal detector had attracted an audience of neighbourhood cats, and meanwhile, I was no closer to the clue. When did you manage to bury all these, Finn?!

But, just then, as I took a break to catch my breath, I felt it again. That same feeling I'd had in the car park

after football … like something wasn't right. Like …
someone was watching me. I turned my head, slowly,
and there was a rustling from the bushes. I stood still,
barely breathing, because I wanted to hear. And I did
hear … footsteps. I crept to the edge of the garden, just
by the wall, and looked down the road. The street lamps
illuminated patches of the pavement and parked cars,
and there, towards the end of the street, someone was
standing, silhouetted against the orange light. Someone
who was about my height, and about my build, and I'm
pretty sure they were looking in my direction. "Finn?!"
I called out.

The figure scuttled off, fast, so fast, disappearing into
the shadows and then … gone.

I ran down the street, looking. I was not going to
give up that easily. "Finn?!" I yelled. "Finn! Please!"

But you didn't call back, and you didn't come back,
and maybe it wasn't you, but I just felt sure that it was,
and I don't know why I started crying. I guess I was
frustrated with the task you'd set me, and hopeful I'd
found you, but then disappointed, and totally confused.

I trudged back home and picked up the metal

detector again. You clearly didn't want me to find you until exactly the right moment, for whatever reason, so there was no choice but to carry on. I wiped my tears away and started sweeping the ground again, and it wasn't long before the familiar high-pitched squeal happened again. This time, I dug down to find a bigger box than the rest.

"Finally!" I muttered.

I pulled it out of the earth, wiped it down, and prised it open. And inside... I mean, I cannot be cross about this – although I am also cross – but this was kind of amazing, and very thoughtful of you, Finn: inside were some trainers.

A present! Some cool kicks. Make sure you wear them ALWAYS. That's an order.

I pulled them on right away since it was an "order".

I was really pleased with them. With my pink hair, and now these, I was so close to no longer being a Massive Great Dork. It was then I noticed a second note in the box:

Hey, handsome! So, things are about to get seriously FUN. But for this, I needed to make sure you have some kind of old wizard-type person to help you on the rest of the quest. Like, you might need a car and things, and we know how stressed you get about anything on wheels – LOL – remember?! Anyhoo – use the mobile I gave you and message the number on the back of this note. Your carriage awaits!

Over and out!

Finn XX

P.S. Your hair looks gorgeous, it really suits you. XXX

I laughed. "Roger that!" I said, doing a little salute.

Hmm. My carriage awaits, does it? That sounds like I'm gonna be going somewhere, and I've no idea how that could happen with my gran visiting tomorrow. You know how she likes to grill me about everything I'm doing wrong and all the bad choices I'm making, Finn. I sure hope you've thought this through...

I pulled the phone out of my pocket and sent the text:

> Hello, Old Wizard? This is Eric. Please bring
> your carriage!

I smiled at the memory of "anything on wheels" stressing me out and then smiled more at the fact you said my hair suited me. Feels like old times, the way you're bantering with me in these notes. Almost like the bad words didn't happen. You know what, Finn? When I see you again, I kinda feel like everything's gonna be OK between us. And as I'm sitting in bed writing this update, I'm still smiling – because the day that happens, well, it's gonna be a very good day.

CHAPTER FOURTEEN

Wednesday, 8 a.m.

"I know what you've done, Eric."

My eyelids fluttered open as I woke from a very pleasant dream (about nachos) to find the figure of my mother looming over my bed.

She had her hands on her hips, Finn. Never a good sign.

Also, bit of a problem, I'd done quite a lot of things recently, so I wasn't sure what she was referring to and didn't want to incriminate myself needlessly. Literally, this could just have been about me forgetting to flush the toilet.

"Can you be more specific?" I asked, attempting my best sweet smile.

"The lawn," she said grimly.

Oh heck.

"After last time, I installed a security camera…"

Oh boy.

"Because I didn't trust that it wasn't one of the neighbours… When I saw the state of the garden this morning, I reviewed the footage, and what did I see…"

I was dead.

"You, Eric, digging up the lawn." She sat down on the edge of my bed. "I'll let you explain in your own words." She looked me straight in the eyes, unblinking and cold.

I swallowed, my mouth dry as sand. You didn't account for my mum installing security, did you, Finn?! What now? If I didn't come up with a good answer, she would ground me for good. What would happen to our adventure then?

Oh *god*, I was going to have to … *improvise.*

"Yes," I said, completely not knowing where I was going with this. "Yes, it was me. I was the one who dug up the lawn. I admit it."

"I know that, Eric, it's clearly you on the video footage."

I nodded. "Yes. But criminals get less time in prison if they plead guilty, right?"

Mum narrowed her eyes at me. "Why, Eric?"

I swallowed again. *Think, Eric, think!* "OK. So. It was because..." My face broke into a smile when I remembered. This wouldn't be entirely the truth, but it also wasn't completely a lie...

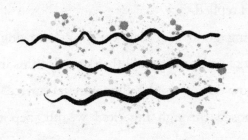

It was the first week of Year 7 and we were set a project to create a time capsule filled with stuff that would be interesting to dig up and discover in six years' time, when we would be in Year 13. We worked in pairs to create our capsules, and, of course, I worked with you, Finn. A lot of groups put in things such as newspapers, books, memory sticks loaded with documents and photos, and even fashions of the day – like a T-shirt.

You were more pragmatic. Reminding me that prices increase over time, you convinced me we should fill our capsule with confectionary, aiming to sell it in six years' time, and making a tidy profit in the process.

"I reckon we'll at least double our money, Eric, if not quadruple it, the way things currently are!" you'd said, grinning.

"Shouldn't we just do what everyone else is doing, though?" I replied.

"Nothing good ever happened by following the crowd, Eric! Trust me, you'll thank me for this in the future. How do you think billionaires get started?"

I supposed through inherited wealth, nepotism, luck, or a lot of socio-economic privilege, but maybe you had a point. You gotta start somewhere.

It only occurred to me months later, when the capsules were buried in a corner of the school field, that all our confectionary would be well past their best before dates when we dug them up.

"Doesn't matter!" you declared. "People pay a fortune for retro stuff on eBay – we'll still be quids in!"

Finn Jones. Every cloud always has a silver lining.

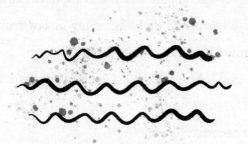

"Finn and I made a time capsule!" I blurted out to Mum, hoping I could adapt the truth convincingly. "Years ago. It was full of stuff ... so someone in the future could dig it up and they'd know about us ... what we read, the music we liked ... that sort of thing. We buried it ... in the garden. And I wasn't supposed to, but I wanted to remember things about Finn, so I ... I dug it up, Mum. Only, I couldn't quite remember where it was, so I had to do a lot of digging."

"Oh, Eric," Mum said, sighing.

"I know. I'm sorry. I'll reflect on what I've done."

Mum leaned forward and wrapped me in her arms. "You know, Eric, it's hard when you lose someone, and

I think maybe it's time I—"

I'll never know what Mum was about to say because she was interrupted by hammering at our front door and shouts of "Jennifer? JENNIFER?!"

"Oh god," Mum hissed. "She's here! Your father's mother!"

"You mean ... Gran?"

"I can think of several other things to call her!" Mum grimaced. "Why can't she see you when you visit your dad?"

I shrugged. "She always likes to see me on the third Saturday of the month, and since Dad's away this month..."

Just then there was a loud bang that sounded a lot like a gunshot, and we heard my gran scream.

OK, she might have been super annoying, but she was still my gran, and it sounded like she'd just been assassinated, so I didn't think twice. I bolted downstairs in just my boxers and the new trainers that you now insist I always wear, Finn, and ran out the front door.

And there was Gran, standing in the middle of the wrecked garden, staring at my aunt Caz, who had just turned up in her clapped-out camper van with the exhaust that always backfires. Aunt Caz is Mum's younger sister, and Gran absolutely hates her because she's a vegetarian environmental protester who sometimes glues herself to petrol tankers.

Gran stared at me. "Eric! Your hair!" she said.

"Cool, huh?"

She looked me up and down and shook her head. "Put your nipples away, young man, it's positively indecent."

Just as I was covering my indecent nipples with my two index fingers, Aunt Caz hooted the horn of the camper van, leapt out, and strode into our garden.

"Oh no, what's she doing here now?" Mum muttered, as she emerged from the house too.

Today, along with her usual pierced nose, Aunt Caz had green hair and was wearing baggy jeans and a T-shirt which had "Rebel" written across the front. "Looking fiiiine, Eric, dude!" she yelled.

"He most certainly does not," Gran replied.

"Mags," Aunt Caz said, nodding at Gran.

"It's Margaret," Gran sniffed.

"Hi, Caz," Mum said warily. "What a surprise! I thought we'd be seeing you next Saturday. I'm not sure this is the best time for an impromptu visit!"

Aunt Caz glanced around the garden. "Loving that you've ditched the lawn and rewilded this whole place, Jen. Trust me, this is what everyone needs to do."

Gran gave a disdainful snort.

"I'm here to pick up Eric," Aunt Caz continued, "so go and get some clothes on, honey, and pack a few more – we need to get going!"

"Where are we going?" I asked, utterly panicked because this was the first I'd heard about any of this, and why did I need to pack? Was this an overnight thing? Would I need toothpaste?

"Hang on!" Gran said. "*I'm* here to see Eric. It's been arranged! I've travelled all the way from Ashby-de-la-Zouch!"

Aunt Caz gave Gran what I would call a sarcastic smile – nice on the outside, but you could tell she wanted to murder her. "Well, *this* has been arranged too." She gave me a wink.

"But what is it?" I bleated.

"Meditation and mindfulness camp," she replied. "You know, aligning your chakras."

"Ahhh, *what?!*" I said.

"There's nothing wrong with Eric's chakras!" Gran huffed. She turned to my mum. "Jennifer? You need to put your foot down."

"Actually," Mum said, "maybe this is a good thing?" She smiled at me sadly. "Maybe this would ... do you good? Give you some time to ... think? About things? That have happened... Focusing on spirituality can really help sometimes, and—"

"Honestly, I'm good!" I chirped.

"Oh yes, Eric's fully zen," Gran agreed. "So zen he's horizontal most of the time ... lazing about in bed. If anything, Eric could do with being a bit *less* zen, and a bit more *get up and go!*"

There she went, already having a pop at me!

"Eric," Aunt Caz said, staring at me with wide eyes –
like, a really meaningful stare. "Let's discuss this on the
way; it's getting late. Chop, chop, go pack!"

"But I can't go to meditation camp!" I wailed. "I'm …
waiting for someone. Someone important."

"Yeah, *me!*" Aunt Caz said. She waved her mobile in
the air. "Finn set this up. Meditation camp? His idea."

I stared at her. Aunt Caz was my wise old mentor?
But meditation camp? Why on earth would you arrange
something so utterly dreadful, Finn? You'd promised
"fun". I couldn't understand it.

"Such a thoughtful boy," Mum said, shaking her
head and wiping away a tear. "Well, now you really
have to go, Eric."

I guess I did if this was part of the plan.

"Caz?" Mum asked. "This place is safe, right? All
insured and properly audited?"

"So safe!" Caz beamed. "I will personally ensure
Eric's safety, don't worry."

Mum nodded, apparently satisfied, so I guessed that
was that.

"Well, how long am I going to be away for? Pants for

how many days?" I asked.

Aunt Caz shrugged. "Seven? I dunno. It doesn't matter; people always stress about packing, but there are always options if you forget things. Would you believe I make a lot of my own clothes from upcycled hessian sacking?"

"Yes, I would," said Gran in a flat voice.

Yeah, that's the thing about Aunt Caz – she's definitely the most chilled and nicest member of my family, but she's also got some "interesting" ideas about things, including a total lack of appreciation for how, if you're going away, you need to know what to take! Seriously, did I need meditation gear? What even was that? Would towels be provided? Did I need smart clothes for the evening? Would there be a formal dinner? How many types of shoes? Would there be a pool? Did I need my Crocs? How about shower gel, or would there be some of that in a dispenser in the bathroom? And if so, would it by hypoallergenic? (You know I have sensitive skin, Finn.)

Total nightmare. In the end, I took all options, and managed to fit everything into a huge case that was almost as tall as I was and weighed twice what I did.

Aunt Caz wasn't happy about it, but what was I supposed to do?

Mum gave me a peck on the cheek and told me to keep in touch, even if it was just a text, and that I should "open my mind and enjoy the experience".

Yeah, right.

I left Mum arguing with Gran about me going off like this and got in the back of Aunt Caz's camper van ... which is when I saw him and screamed.

CHAPTER FIFTEEN

Wednesday, 8.30 a.m.

"Eric? Are you all right?" Mum shouted across from the garden, having heard my scream.

"Fine! It's nothing!" I shouted back, rolling down the window. "I'm just super excited about camp!" I rolled the window back up and glanced down. "What are you doing here?" I hissed.

Cooper gave me a toothy grin from where he was hiding on the floor. "Obviously I'm coming too. I'm your wingman, remember?"

"Are you good at yoga and all that jazz?"

"Yeah, we're not going to meditation camp," Aunt Caz said, firing up the engine with a roar. "That was just to throw them off the scent!"

With that, Aunt Caz tooted the horn and we drove away, Cooper heaving himself off the floor and into the seat beside me once we'd rounded the corner and were safely out of sight, while I just sat there with my mind blown about what the heck was going on and had I, in fact, packed all the wrong gear ... even though I had practically *all* my gear with me.

It was then that Aunt Caz passed a note back to me. "This is literally all Finn gave me. I know nothing else, except he gave me petrol money to pay for this part of the trip."

"Where did he get all the cash from?"

Aunt Caz shrugged, so I turned my attention to the note:

If you're reading this you are now hopefully on your way to "meditation camp". I knew that was the only way I had any hope of convincing your mum to let you come on this ROOOOOAD TRIIIIIP! Woo hoo!! Now, Eric, I know you so well ... and I know all this random, unplanned adventure will be causing you a *lot of stress. So I'm gonna be kind. You're in control, OK? For this next bit, you have completely free choice. Just follow what I've written on the back of this note and pick your answers. I'm not influencing you in any way. Choose whatever you like. Over and out, Finn X*

"Roger that," I muttered, turning the paper over and glancing at the words. Ohh, I knew what this was. This was a mind-reading trick. You, Finn Jones, seriously reckoned that whenever you put this adventure together, you *knew* how I was going to respond and what I was going to pick, did you?

Sure, you know me well.

But not *that* well.

I was intrigued, though. I wanted to know how you'd manage to pull this one off, so I handed the paper to Cooper and told him to read.

"Okaaaay," Cooper said, following the text. "Think of a three-digit number, but make sure each digit is different. And Finn reminds you, you have total free choice here. You're in control, he says."

"432," I said. "No! Wait, I've changed my mind. 875."

"Sure?"

"Sure. I just changed at the last minute to trick Finn," I explained.

"OK. Reverse the digits."

"So that's now 578."

"Subtract the smaller number from the larger number." Cooper handed me his phone. "Here, use the calculator. I know maths isn't your…"

"Ooh, *burn!*" (But, also, seriously – how dare he!)

"Well, anyway, doesn't matter, just use it to be accurate," Cooper muttered.

"Thanks, OK, so 875 minus 578. That equals 297."

"Now reverse the digits of that number too."

"792."

"Now add that to the number before it was reversed."

I tapped at the calculator. "297 add 792. So that's 1089."

"OK. Finn's last instruction is to find the book *A Monster Calls* which he's hidden in the glove compartment. He says take the first three digits, and that's your page number, and the last digit is the line number."

"So that's page 108, line 9," I said. "Aunt Caz? Can you pull over and look in the glove compartment?"

Aunt Caz parked up in a side road and leaned across, fiddling in the compartment on the passenger side. "Where did *this* come from?" she asked, pulling *A Monster Calls* out.

"Finn," I said taking it from her. I flicked to page 108, line 9 and…

I froze.

How. Did. You. Do. It?

Because there, on page 108, line 9, the text had been blanked out with Tippex, and over it had been written, in your unmistakable handwriting, Finn:

Head to Snappy Snaps on the high street.
Pick up my order. (And also, read this book
sometime, it's great.)

Free choice. I'd picked that first number myself – or so I'd thought. And somehow you were still one step ahead of me, Finn. I didn't even want to know how. This just confirmed everything I already knew: that you were some kind of wizard and whatever you had planned, it was epic and it was out-of-this-world special, and there was no way someone like you could be anything other than alive.

'Cause magic just doesn't die.

It lives.

And so do you.

"To Snappy Snaps!" I shouted. (And don't get me wrong, I'd rather that had been something a little more dramatic – "To New York!" or "To the secret laboratory!" perhaps – but if you had planned it, then Snappy Snaps was good enough for me!)

CHAPTER SIXTEEN

Wednesday, 9.30 a.m.

I spread out the photographs on the table in Starbucks – because, *thank you, Finn*, as well as leaving the pictures for us to collect, you'd also left a fully charged Starbucks card, so now we were all sitting over the road from Snappy Snaps sipping caramel Frappuccinos.

I guess you thought we'd need some refreshments by this point, plus some sugar for brain power to work out the next clue.

There were four photos in total. The first three all seemed linked. The fourth was a photo of Britney Steers – the awesome go-kart that we built when we entered the soap box derby earlier this year. It made me smile when I saw that, but I wasn't sure what relevance

it had to the other photos.

"Look how happy Finn looks in that photo!" Cooper said, indicating the one of you in a harness.

I took the picture and traced my finger over your face. You did look happy, Finn. Ecstatic, actually. Like you were having one of the best days of your life. When was it taken? One thing was for sure: you looked a hell of a lot better than you did when I last saw you … a lot less sleepy, your eyes sparkling like they usually sparkled. That was definitely a good sign.

"Jolly Valley," Cooper said, pointing to the sign on the cabin in the first photo. "That's the best clue we have, right?"

I was already on my phone, as the internet was our best bet here. I scrolled through the search results then clicked on a link and –

Oh my actual heck.

No, no, no, no, no.

"Are you OK, Eric?" Aunt Caz asked. "You've gone very pale."

"Jolly Valley," I said, reading the text on the website, "is famous for having Europe's longest, highest zip wire, nine hundred metres long, with a vertical drop of over six hundred metres, across the infamous Devil's Gorge." I blinked at everyone, an ice chill prickling up my spine. "Longest? Highest? Six-hundred-metre drop? *Devil's* Gorge? Since when was anything named *that* a good thing? And why is it 'infamous'? Infamous for *what*? People dying?!"

"Calm down, Eric, I'm sure it's fine," Aunt Caz said.

"Really?" I said, as I googled "how safe are zip wires?". "According to this, zip wires are *generally* safe. *Generally* isn't the same as 'totally'."

"Is anything totally safe?" Aunt Caz said.

"Yes," I replied. "Knitting is pretty safe, for example."

"You could get stabbed by a needle, though," Cooper mused.

"Shut up, Coops. That's ridiculous." I scrolled some more. "Researchers at Ohio State University found that almost twelve per cent of zip-wire incidents resulted in fractures or other injuries that required hospitalization…"

"Eric, this isn't helpful," Aunt Caz said.

"You *have* to know what you're getting into," I

replied. "And listen to this! In 2015, a twelve-year-old girl at a YMCA camp in North Carolina died after her tether snapped over a twelve-metre canyon. The same year, an eighteen-year-old man in Tennessee died after a gruesome fall when his neck became entangled in the safety harness. Last May, a woman died at Raindance Mountain Resort after colliding with a falling tree. In August 2016…"

"Shall we just not do it then?" Cooper said.

Aunt Caz put her drink down firmly. "You *have* to do it. And look!" she added, pointing to the third photo. "Finn clearly did it. If Finn did it…"

"*Of course!*" I muttered, realizing. "The fourth photo!"

"Oh yeah." Cooper frowned, picking up the one featuring Britney Steers. "What's this one about anyway?"

I took a deep breath. "Let me explain."

Cooper frowned. "Why are you waving your arms around all weirdly?"

"It's a flashback, Cooper!"

IN CASE, LIKE COOPER,
YOU DON'T KNOW THIS YET,
THIS IS A
FLASH BACK!!

It was our biggest challenge yet ... the soap box derby!
Twenty teams, twenty home-made karts, and one race
down the big hill in town with one kart crowned the
winner. For weeks, Finn and I had planned, sketched,
sawn wood and screwed on wheels, until finally we'd
made...

Britney Steers!

(All the karts had to have names that were puns,
you see?)

Britney could hold only one person, was made
from a very light wood to minimize the weight, had a
steering system that we'd tinkered around with forever
to get right, and cool wheels, which we'd got off eBay.
Here was the thing: I was lighter, so it made sense for
me to drive the kart. But I was TERRIFIED. It's not that
I didn't trust our ability as go-kart engineers – although,

truth be told, I didn't really – it was just such a steep hill, and there was so much risk involved. What if the steering broke, and I smacked straight into a wall? What if I was catapulted out, hit my head and got brain damage? Accidents happen all the time – as Mum always reminds me – so why put yourself at any extra risk?

Well, long story short, I backed out of driving Britney Steers after googling about go-kart crashes and seeing my fears were totally founded.

Anyway. It was the day of the go-kart race and the anticipation had reached fever pitch. We'd even chased away a couple of spies trying to find out exactly what Finn and I were tinkering with in his garage. The truth was, I didn't even know – it was Finn with the spanners and the screwdrivers, making fine adjustments to the steering column and the wheels, while I occasionally held bolts for him, nodded along while he talked, pretending I understood, or just kept us hydrated with orange squash and fed with chocolate and peanut butter cookies I'd baked that morning.

"It's about balance," Finn said. "Thicker tyres give us

more grip and control, but thinner means less friction, which means more speed. You gotta balance the two."

Honestly, I had no idea, I just loved how he knew things. I offered up the plate of cookies; they were the best I could contribute to this partnership, since I wouldn't drive and didn't know anything about engineering.

"Is it OK if I save it for after the race?" Finn said. He patted his tummy. "The less weight we're carrying the better!"

Finn was all about the speed. And, to me, that spelled DANGER. "Are you absolutely sure this is a good idea?" I asked.

Finn shrugged. "What's the worst that could happen?"

"You could crash, break your neck and be paralyzed."

"That's not the worst that could happen."

"OK, then, you could crash and actually die."

"That's not the worst that could happen either."

"Then what, Finn? What could be worse than that?"

He put his spanner down, turned to me and squeezed my shoulder. "The worst that could happen is that I don't do it at all, never have this amazing experience, and regret it for the rest of my life."

Later that afternoon, as I stood at the bottom of the huge hill, I watched Finn take the lead, expertly handling Britney Steers, and as he whooshed past me, heading at high speed for a prickly hedge and a ditch full of stagnant water, I saw the look in his eyes, and it was exhilaration and hysteria and pure joy, and I wished I'd had the guts to go through with it because it looked like the best thing ever.

I waved my arms about.

"Is that the end of the flashback, or is this now a flashback within a flashback?" Cooper asked.

"End of flashback," I said. "So, you see? That photo is Finn reminding me that I chickened out of driving *Britney* and regretted it, so I shouldn't repeat the same mistake. Regardless of the risks."

I chewed my lip in thought. *Very clever,* Finn. And I knew you were right, although that didn't make me feel much better.

"And for whatever reason," I continued, "Finn needs us to go down the zip wire at Jolly Valley. It's part of his plan. And I just have to trust him."

Aunt Caz clapped her hands together. "Well, it's a long drive. I suggest we set off now, camp overnight, and we can be there for tomorrow morning."

"Camping?" I said weakly. "But I haven't brought a tent!"

Aunt Caz smiled. "We can sleep under the stars!"

"What about bears?!"

"You know we're in England, don't you?" She laughed.

"Don't fret, Eric. I was joking – I packed tents."

I snapped my fingers. "Planning! I like it!"

"I know you do." Aunt Caz sighed.

We finished our drinks and headed outside. We were walking back to the van when it hit me again. That *feeling*. Something was amiss. It felt like … I should be noticing something, that something was right in front of my eyes, and I needed to see it, but I couldn't. I looked around… People, parked cars, a bus, a woman with a clipboard trying to stop people to do a survey, one of those street entertainers who magically hover above the ground, frozen solid. Everything seemed pretty much normal. Was I just imagining things?

"Let's avoid the clipboard lady," I said, guiding everyone across the road. "She'll just try to ask us things and we've no time for that."

It wasn't until we were back in the van and on our way that I realized something.

I'd just told a story about us, and I'd told it to Cooper and Aunt Caz, and not to you, and that felt a bit weird, but it also didn't feel completely wrong.

I hope you don't mind, Finn.

CHAPTER SEVENTEEN

Wednesday, 10.30 p.m.

Writing this in my sleeping bag, next to Cooper in our tent. He's asleep now, but I've had a bit of a row with him.

We drove for hours, before Aunt Caz found somewhere we could camp for the night. It wasn't a designated campsite, it was basically a random field next to some woods, so there was no running water – which meant, of course, no toilets.

"What if we need to use the lavatory?" I asked, by which I meant I *need to use the lavatory*, and not just for a wee, so this was already feeling super awkward.

And that was how I ended up squatting over a hole in the ground that I'd had to dig myself behind some bushes, accidentally stung my bare arse on a nettle, and I think that's what set me off on my bad mood.

The second thing was that there was no phone reception since we were in the middle of nowhere, and I really needed to message Mum to let her know I was OK. (Hopefully she isn't panicking, although I kind of know she must be. I just hope I can text her from Jolly Valley tomorrow.)

We were also all really tired by this point, *and* hungry.

Which leads on to the final irritating thing: for dinner, Aunt Caz made her "famous" five bean chilli. I'm not saying the chilli wasn't nice (although it wasn't nice), but the fact is, if you put two boys in a tent who have both eaten considerable quantities of beans, there's going to be a certain level of gas produced, and right now, if anyone lit a match, this place would go up like a rocket.

So we were both lying here, with sore stomachs from all the gas building up inside us, and neither of us could sleep. And that's when Cooper started asking me things.

"I'm curious. Finn was pretty fearless, right?"

"Sure," I said.

"Was he scared of anything? What about spiders?"

"Nah, he loves critters."

"Ghosts, vampires or mind flayers?"

"Don't bother him."

"Bananas?"

I sat up. "Coops? What the hell? Why would he be scared of bananas?"

Cooper shrugged. "Some people have irrational phobias. I've heard some people are scared of bananas. I think it's the texture, or smell, or something."

"Well, Finn's chill about all fruits. And vegetables, for that matter. I'm not saying he *likes* eating them, but he's definitely not afraid of them."

Cooper whistled. "He genuinely wasn't scared of anything."

"Well," I said. "More or less."

I thought for a moment, then became aware of Cooper just staring at me. "It's nothing, forget it," I muttered.

"Tell me. I'd like to know."

I swallowed. I wasn't sure this was my story to tell, but it had been bugging me for a while, and maybe if I told Coops, I'd feel better about it, like how telling him the story of Britney Steers had made me feel a bit better. "OK, well … *flashback…*"

We both waved our arms around.

Finn had been feeling weird for a while. He'd kept on at his mum, saying he should go to the doctor's to get checked out, but I think she just thought he was trying to get out of school because he had a maths test, or something. Then, after he crashed Britney Steers, he started feeling dizzy. Everyone reckoned it was mild concussion, so he went to A&E to make sure. I didn't hear from him for ages after that, and I was getting a bit worried, 'cause he wasn't replying to my messages either, but two days later he did finally message me, and

I went round to his house. I noticed how tired his mum looked when she let me in, and as I passed the lounge, I could see there were a load of other adults in there, all sitting quietly, which was weird, because Finn's house was usually loud and fun. I bounded up the stairs and into Finn's room, where he was sitting cross-legged on his bed.

"Guess what, Eric?" he said. "Turns out I was right, I *am* sick."

I grinned, because I was sure this was a set-up for one of his jokes. "What's up? Allergic to school, are you? That would be a real trag—"

"No, it's a bit more serious, Eric. They did some tests at the hospital. And some scans."

He looked at me with wide eyes, and, for the first time ever, I saw something in them I'd never seen before.

Fear.

He swallowed. "I'm going to need some time off school. And they've got medicine they can give me. It's horrible medicine by all accounts, makes you feel like the arse end of a donkey" – he tried to laugh – "but it's meant to help."

I stared at him. "So ... you'll be OK? They can make you better?"

"Hopefully." He swallowed again and looked away.

"Finn?" I said, sitting down on the bed next to him "They can make you better, right? The doctors?"

He looked back at me and nodded. "Yeah. I mean, a lot of people get better from this thing. But some people ... well, some people don't."

"But you'll be in the first category. The people who *do* get better, so that's fine."

"But what if I'm not?"

The way he just said that, so direct; my mouth opened, but no words came out. I'd never seen Finn like this before. He was always so positive. Always so sure things would work out OK. Always a silver lining.

"Exactly," Finn said, referring to the stunned expression on my face.

"No, wait! It'll be fine, of course it will!"

"Easy for you to say, Eric!" he snapped. "*You'll* be fine ... you'll still get to do everything. See the world, whatever. Bad luck for me, huh? I mean, *whatever*, but you can't just sit there and tell me it'll all be OK, 'cause it might not be, not for me anyway."

I stared at him. I didn't know what to say. I didn't know how to help. In my heart, I knew he wasn't really angry at me, he was angry at the situation, and, more than that, he was *scared*. This was the one thing Finn was afraid of. *Not being here.* But right then I was worried anything I did say would only make things worse.

"Do you want me to go?" I muttered.

"Go if you want!"

"Well ... what do you want?"

"Oh, Eric, just go. Go on. You don't understand."

So I did. I went.

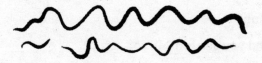

"End of flashback, Coops."

"Poor Finn," Cooper said. "He was scared, and he took it out on you."

"You think?"

"Yeah, of course," Cooper said. "He didn't mean it. That's not who Finn was, was it? I can't even imagine you two arguing like that."

I sighed. "Oh, that was nothing. You should have seen the time when—" I glanced at Cooper, who had his eyebrows raised, waiting for *that* story. I looked away quickly. "Doesn't matter. That's not important. All that really matters is that we find Finn."

This silence hung in the air for what felt like ages.

"Eric," Cooper said softly. "Finn's ... not coming back. You know that, right? You do know that he's ... well, he's gone now."

Cooper reached out to me, I think to put his hand on my shoulder, but I batted him away. "Did you see him?" I asked.

"Huh?"

"Did you see him? In the coffin?"

"Well ... no."

"Did you ever see his body?"

"No, of course not, that's not really—"

"So, OK, then how do you know? How do you know he's gone?"

"Because—"

"Stop!" I said. "Just stop. And think. With Finn, things

aren't always what they seem. You can't take anything for granted. And just because some people say things are a certain way, it doesn't always mean they are. You have to think things through yourself. I know Finn was sick. I know that. But I also know he would have found a way out of it. I may not know how exactly, but I know he has."

But Cooper wouldn't shut up. "I wish that was true as well, OK, Eric? I wish it was true, but—"

"YOU'VE NEVER HAD AS GOOD A FRIEND AS FINN SO YOU HAVE NO IDEA! YOU'RE A FRIENDLESS LOSER! SO JUST LEAVE IT, COOPER! IF YOU DON'T BELIEVE IN HIM THEN WHY ARE YOU EVEN HERE?"

Cooper just stared at me, looking kind of stunned, while I immediately regretted my words – something which felt horribly familiar. But something inside me wouldn't let me apologize … which also felt horribly familiar. Cooper just turned over in his sleeping bag, curled up, and went to sleep – or at least is pretending to be.

I'll make it up to him in the morning. That is something I will definitely do. I've learned that lesson.

And then I'm going to go down that zip wire, just like you want me to, and I'll be one step closer to finding you, and Cooper will finally see why I'm so frustrated with everyone. No fear. No regrets. Not ever.

Goodnight, Finn.

Over and out. Roger that! I love ya.

CHAPTER EIGHTEEN

Thursday, 8 a.m.

I got up super early while Cooper was still sleeping (and farting!) so I could collect some wildflowers in order to present him with an apology bouquet when he woke up. This was something Dad used to do for Mum, and while it certainly didn't save *their* relationship, I was hopeful it might help with me and Coops. Truth is, I actually quite like him, and while he's no you, Finn, he didn't deserve my harsh words last night. Cooper's one of the good guys.

And maybe we say things we don't mean when we're scared.

"With my humble apologies," I said, offering the bouquet the moment Cooper crawled out of our tent.

Cooper rubbed sleep from his eyes, stretched, yawned and took the bouquet, which I'd hand-tied with the elastic from my boxers. On reflection, it wasn't the best choice since that had rendered them "comedy falling-down pants", but it was the best I could do.

"Are those nettles?" Cooper asked.

"Yes. It needed some green."

"And … foxgloves?" He frowned. "You know they're poisonous, right?"

"Wow, Cooper, yes, I do know, but you're not eating the bouquet, you're just looking at it!"

Cooper nodded. "Like a sort of … 'Danger Bouquet'! I like it!"

"Do you?"

Cooper cracked a smile. "It's OK, Eric. I'm not angry with you. You're upset, I get that."

So that was all easier than I expected.

And I wondered, *would it have been like that if I'd just apologized to Finn when I—*

I shook the memory away. Not now. There was Devil's Gorge to conquer.

As we drove on, I waited for any bars of reception to

appear on my mobile. Finn – I waited a whole *hour*, and then, finally, one little bar flashed up.

"Finally!" I said.

A barrage of messages started pinging up on my phone, all from Mum, with increasing levels of panic and hysteria concerning my whereabouts.

Ahh, man.

I had a feeling the reception wouldn't last long, as we were trundling through tiny lanes surrounded by hills. As quickly as I could, I hammered out a quick message to Mum, just a single word, just to put her mind at rest:

Hello!

Unfortunately, it autocorrected just as I pressed send, so what it actually read was:

Help!

And then all the bars disappeared. "Aaarghh! *Seriously?!*" I muttered. Maybe it hadn't sent? Or maybe Mum got it and we'd have a laugh about it later. I'd try again as soon as I could.

We reached Jolly Valley a couple of hours later. From the screams of people going down the zip wire, "jolly" seemed a bit of a stretch. Horror Valley might have been more appropriate, or Pee Your Pants Canyon … and yet every single person there seemed super excited and enthusiastic.

I checked out the set-up. It was actually a dual zip wire, which meant you could go down with someone else. You were each attached to a harness thing, which appeared to mean you couldn't actually fall, although who knew if it was really safe?

I had a peek over the edge. Big mistake. I couldn't do it, couldn't do it, couldn't do it…

"Eric?"

I whipped around to find a man in a yellow polo shirt with "Jolly Valley" embroidered on it.

"How did you know my name?"

The man looked panicked for a moment, then smiled. "I have this for you." And he handed me an envelope.

OK, that was weird, but I could worry about it later. I ripped the envelope open and found your next note:

OK, Eric – here's my advice: don't google how safe this is, OK? (I say that knowing you already have, of course!) Just know that no one has died on this particular zip wire. (At the time of writing this.) And that's good! Also, there have been no life-changing injuries. So that's also good! So it's all good and the risk of fractured or broken bones is really low, or slightly more than low, like maybe more like medium, but still pretty on the low side. Also, life is full of risks, but hey, what's the worst that could happen, right?! ENJOY! Over and out! Finn x

"Roger that," I replied, shaking my head. Thought you could panic me, huh, Finn? I know your game! I loved that you were winding me up, knowing that, of course, I would go through with this. Cooper, on the other hand, who had read the note over my shoulder, completely flipped out.

"It's OK, Coops," I said, trying to reassure him. "The note is saying that it's actually pretty safe."

"Is it? Because the only words I'm seeing are 'died', 'injuries', 'fractured' and 'risk'." He gulped. "Oh god, I really need the toilet."

And off he ran.

I must have got reception again, because my mobile suddenly started ringing. It was Mum.

"Ready?" yellow polo shirt man asked.

I declined her call. I'd have to ring her back at the bottom. Then I glanced at the platform, and even just doing that made my stomach do flips. I'd told myself it would be fine; I'd remembered how much I regretted not driving Britney Steers that day, but even so, I really needed you right then, Finn. I was terrified. If anyone was going to be able to help me do this, it was you. It was like you'd set this up, but then left me with no help, because Cooper was quite clearly useless.

"You need to hurry up," the man continued. "It's just, there's someone waiting at the other end for you. And I think it's going to be a pretty big surprise."

And just like that, Finn, you *did* help me, didn't you?

You epic, hilarious, awesome genius!

Because waiting at the bottom…

Was going to be you.

CHAPTER NINETEEN

Thursday, 11 a.m.

Once Cooper had been coaxed out of the toilet and into his harness, we stood on the platform, and I won't lie, we were both bricking it. Man, it was high. Like, sure, it seemed safe (as far as clinging to a single thin metal wire over a six-hundred-metre drop can be safe), and loads of people had been down the wire before us, but it was terrifying knowing that, if something did go wrong, it would probably be curtains.

"Sorry, I just stress-farted," Cooper muttered.

"Same," I admitted.

But we needed to get down there. Because down there was you, Finn. Finally, the ultimate prize was just moments away! It took one minute to descend to the other side. Only sixty seconds. I just needed to pluck up the courage, and that meant plucking up Cooper's courage, because everything is easier as a pair.

So, I tried to think what you would tell me, Finn, if it was you up here, and I think you'd be proud: "Cooper, we're going to jump together, at the same time, me and you, a team. It's not just *you* jumping, it's *us* jumping, and if we die, we die together, but don't focus on that, focus on how awesome this will be, and not just the thrill and the adrenaline, but the view! Imagine what the view will be like, Coops! High above the trees, high above everything, looking down, as we glide towards the finish line and certain glory – and what could be better than sharing that amazing experience with someone else! With each other! And whatever happens in our lives, Cooper, wherever life may take us, me and you, we'll always have this special moment, this amazing moment; it'll always be ours, and for all those—"

"Are you two lovebirds going down the wire or up the aisle?" yellow polo shirt man asked.

I looked at Cooper. "You ready, buddy?"

He smiled back at me. "Did you just call me 'buddy'?"

"I guess that's what you are, Coops, and I for one—"

Something pushed me, I flew forward, off the platform, hanging in the air and: "ARGHHHHHHH!"

We'd both been pushed off the platform simultaneously by yellow polo shirt man – I mean, COME ON! How can that even be legal?!

"ARRGHHHHHHHHHH!"

And, oh boy, the speed, the wind rushing past, pummelling my face, rocketing forward, while plunging, out of control, everything blurred, heart in my mouth and stomach somewhere doing three-sixty flips, dropping, falling, hurtling, and feeling such terror ... but such *beautiful* terror. Isn't that weird? None of this was horrible. I was *free*. I was *alive*.

We were reaching the finish – I could see another yellow-shirted staff member waiting ahead of us on the ground below – and my heart started beating even harder, because that meant I was going to see you, and suddenly I just wanted the zip wire to end, and even though it was only another fifteen seconds, it felt like eternity.

The moment I was clipped out of my harness, I ran forward, looking for you. I spun around, left and right, back again, but I couldn't see you, and then my mobile started ringing again, and – *ugh!* – it was Mum, so I had to answer, "Hello?" and then, out of nowhere, I was grabbed from behind – by really strong arms – not your arms, adult arms. I twisted and—

And I screamed and dropped my phone, and honestly, I wasn't sure how much more my heart could take at this point. "Who are you? Where's Finn?!" I wailed, as I tried to squirm out of the zombie's grasp. Getting no response, I managed to kick it in the shins, which finally made it drop me. "Where's Finn?" I demanded.

Still no response (other than a swear word and some hopping), but instead the zombie offered me an envelope.

"Another note!" I unclenched my fists, stepped away from the zombie, and sighed. *This had better be* good. I ripped it open.

Eric! Did *you* actually do it then? This was the challenge I was seriously worried about! Cool though, wasn't it? I did this zip wire myself when I was setting all this up for you, and – wow – it's breathtaking on the way down, isn't it?

I found myself nodding along as I read, because, yes, it was, and part of me was seriously happy that you had experienced that exact same thing too, but part of me was also on edge because you'd promised you would be here, waiting for me – so where were you?

Anyway, back to business. Eric Griffin, tomorrow you and Cooper will join forces to fight a ZOMBIE INVASION. This is going to be one epic battle! Eric, I think you should draw this one in your journal – make it like a manga, so it's super cool. And, Eric? Even though I won't be, I'd love it if you could make out like I'm there too – fighting the zombies with you. Will you do that? It'd mean loads if you did. Make me a hero (with big muscles if you can!).

Over and out!

Finn XX

"Roger that!" I snapped back. I had a billion questions – "What do you mean, fight a zombie invasion?!" being one of the bigger ones – but all I really wanted to know right then was where you were, Finn.

"Where is he?!" I demanded, stomping back up to the zombie. "Where's Finn?"

The zombie glanced at Cooper for some reason, then back at me. "Eric … Finn's not here any more. You know that."

I don't know where it came from, but this RAGE bubbled up inside me then; I think it was just the casual, easy way the zombie said you weren't here any more, like it was that simple to explain. I hated it, and I had so much anger and so much fury that I started hitting and kicking the zombie, first in the shins again, then all over his decaying body, and, I dunno, he must have tripped over his battered shoes as he was trying to shield himself from the blows, because I'm sure this wasn't really my fault, but he kind of ended up face down in the mud and I think he sort of knocked himself out.

CHAPTER TWENTY

Thursday, 2 p.m.

"We need to have a talk."

Words that no one wants to hear, ever. Aunt Caz handed me and Cooper mugs of hot chocolate and sat down on one of the folding camping chairs next to me. We'd parked up about half an hour away from Jolly Valley, on an actual campsite this time, not that I was bothered about their on-site swimming pool or amusement arcade. I was still livid about the whole lack-of-Finn situation. Where the hell were you?

"Look, if it's about the zombie, how was I to know he was actually a human dressed up? That's a pretty hard distinction to make when zombies actually are humans who've been bitten and then zombified. Plus,

I didn't mean for him to be knocked out. Plus, the paramedics said he'd be fine. Plus, he agreed not to press charges." I blew out a frustrated breath and sipped my hot chocolate. (It wasn't like your hot chocolate, Finn. No marshmallows, no cream, and no Mars bar stuck in the top of it either. Aunt Caz was an amateur when it came to hot chocolate.)

"Eric, you know the zombie was just another person that Finn had arranged to be part of this whole adventure, right?"

"Sure. Finn's planned it all, I know that."

Aunt Caz nodded. "Exactly. And do you know when he planned it?"

I shrugged. "It must have been after his trip," I said. "Everyone calls it his 'trip of a lifetime' but actually that's when he had his secret cure and he knew he'd have to disappear afterwards because the doctors would start asking questions when he suddenly started to get better and—"

"Eric, that trip was just a nice holiday for Finn – do some stuff he'd never done, and see some places he'd never seen – because the doctors said there was nothing more they could do," Aunt Caz said. "After he'd done that, and before he returned home, he set up this treasure hunt for you. Well, he did most of it then. He visited each location, talked to people, asked them to help, told them why, and they all agreed. I know because that's when he roped me into all this."

"What? That can't be right ... I mean, why would everyone agree?" I asked, my mind spinning, trying to make sense of this news. "Why would all these people help a random kid like Finn? I mean, he's charming, I know that; he's always pretty good at getting his own way, but this seems like a lot."

Aunt Caz squeezed my knee. "Because he was dying, Eric. You don't turn down a dying boy's wishes."

I stared hard into the bubbles on top of my hot chocolate. Every time someone says something like that, it's like they're stabbing me and twisting the knife. I took an unsteady breath. "Don't you see? That was all a cover story. Something amazing happened – something secret – I know it did. And do you know how I know? Finn told me."

I put my drink down and waved my arms about.

"Ooh! Flashback!" Cooper said.

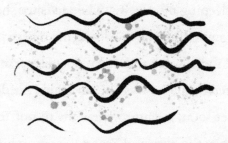

A few weeks after Finn had got back from his so-called "trip of a lifetime" he got taken into hospital because it seemed he was getting sicker – like, more weak, and sometimes he couldn't stand for long. He also had a lot of headaches, and couldn't keep his food down, I was told. The thing was, Finn and I had had a row before he'd gone on the trip – it doesn't matter what about – and we weren't really talking. He hadn't called me while he'd been away on this trip, and I hadn't called him. But hearing Finn wasn't feeling so good made me feel bad for him. And I reckoned it would be good to see him, and maybe be the bigger person and apologize for what happened.

But when I went in, Finn was different. I almost didn't recognize him. A lot of doctors and nurses were fussing around him that day, I remember that, and Finn had been sleeping mostly. But when I visited, he woke up, and he smiled, and he said it was nice to see me. His voice was kind of weak and shaky, not like normal Finn at all. I asked him if he was OK, and said I needed him to get better soon, because we had the rest of Year 7 to face, and then the horror of Year 8.

"Come on, Finn," I said. "I need you with me! Eric and Finn – the dream team! We're gonna take on the world and we're gonna win, remember? Everyone will know our names!"

And I won't ever forget it, because he reached out, and he squeezed my hand and he whispered, "Don't worry, Eric – I've discovered the secret of immortality! I'm gonna be around for a very long time! Everyone is gonna know my name!"

And he smiled at me again, and then his eyelids gently closed, then opened, and then he almost said something else, but didn't. He sighed, squeezed my hand again, and drifted off to sleep.

And I still hadn't apologized to him. There was no point saying it while he was asleep; I needed him to actually hear it. I needed him to *know* it. So, fine, I thought, I'd come the next day and tell him then.

The next day, Mum told me Finn's parents wanted to spend some time alone with him, which was cool because I had extra drama club rehearsals after school anyway.

The day after that … I was woken up by the house phone ringing at six in the morning. And then Mum came into my room, and she said Finn had died.

And I almost believed it, until I remembered what he'd told me, about immortality – and this is Finn we're talking about – and we had plans, and dreams, and we were going to do so much together, and I hadn't had the chance to say sorry yet, and I couldn't leave things like that, and so, you see, it's just not possible.

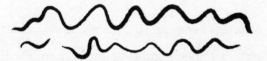

"End of flashback," I said. "Do you see now? Why else would he have been talking about immortality?"

Aunt Caz wiped her eyes. "I don't know, Eric. He would have been on some pretty heavy medication.

Sometimes it can make you say things you don't mean."

I shook my head. "Nah. He knew. He knew exactly what he was saying. And he wanted me to know too. To understand. They found a cure. I reckon his gran smuggled him out of the country. On that day I didn't visit him. That's when it happened. Or they sent some special medicine here instead. You'll see. Everyone will see."

Aunt Caz took a deep breath and regarded me for a long moment, but I couldn't even bring myself to look at her face. "All right. Well, maybe we will. I guess we press on with this thing – like Finn wanted."

Finally! "Yes! Exactly, thank you! We press on. All I have to do is follow Finn's exact instructions. It's so simple. Never know who I might find! Just like Finn says."

"Your mum's been calling," Aunt Caz said, changing the subject. "I've been ignoring her because she'll just ask questions about this meditation camp you're meant to be on that I can't answer." She lowered her voice. "I'm bad at lying. Especially to your mum. She scares me a bit."

"Same!" I chuckled. "I don't want her to tell me to come back. Shall I ignore her too?" I glanced at my phone. Five missed calls from her in the last hour.

"Just message her, Eric. Tell her you're fine."

I hammered out a quick text:

> Hello, hello! All fine here! Enjoying yoga!

I hit send, only to realize later on that (due to autocorrect) what I'd sent was:

> Help, help! A fire here! Employing yoghurt!

Aunt Caz went inside the camper van to read for a bit, leaving me and Cooper sitting outside, finishing our drinks.

"So, ready for a zombie battle?" Cooper asked, grinning. "I mean, you've already knocked one out, so I'm thinking this will be a breeze?"

I winced, then smiled. "Hey, I'm a natural, what can I say? Finn would know exactly how to fight zombies, of course. Like, he'd know all the actual techniques and strategies. He knew how to do *everything*."

A few minutes later, I got a message on the Finn phone with a link to click – and it led me to a web page.

"Finn Jones, you most epic and fabulous of boys!" I said, beaming. How had he done this? How had it arrived *just as we were talking about it*? If Finn wasn't somehow here, how could this happen? "Coops, would you look at this?!"

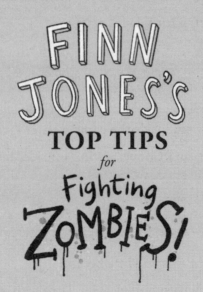

FINN JONES'S **TOP TIPS** *for* Fighting ZOMBIES!

- **Don't fight!** Hand-to-hand combat is NOT ADVISED! If you get bitten, you'll become a zombie too! So keep your distance!

- **Exploit their weaknesses!** Zombies are SLOW and GULLIBLE – it isn't hard to distract them. "Ooh, look! Fresh and tasty brains!" Works every time!

- **Pretend to be a zombie!** Just walk with stiff legs and your arms out while moaning and looking like you just crawled out of bed for school on Monday morning – they'll never guess you aren't one of them!

- **Keep quiet, keep hidden!** Zombies can't find you if they can't see or hear you!

- **RUN!** If all else fails – just run.

(Eric – I highly recommend you save and bookmark this handy guide I've kindly made you. You never know when you might need it, and based on what's been happening in the world in the last few years, I'd say a zombie apocalypse is super likely right now.)

I looked up from the phone screen and smiled. "Do you know what, Coops? I have no idea what's gonna happen tomorrow, no idea what to expect, and normally that would terrify me, but..."

"But?"

I shrugged. "But I'm actually looking forward to this!" I smiled at him. "Literally cannot wait!"

Cooper laughed and I laughed, and for a short moment I forgot about everything, and how much I missed you, and life felt good again and full of possibility.

I hope there are many more moments like that, Finn. Endless moments of feeling good. That's what life should be, right? That's what we deserve. Especially you. After everything.

CHAPTER TWENTY-ONE

Friday, 1 p.m.

Finn Jones, Eric Griffin and Cooper Feldman star in...

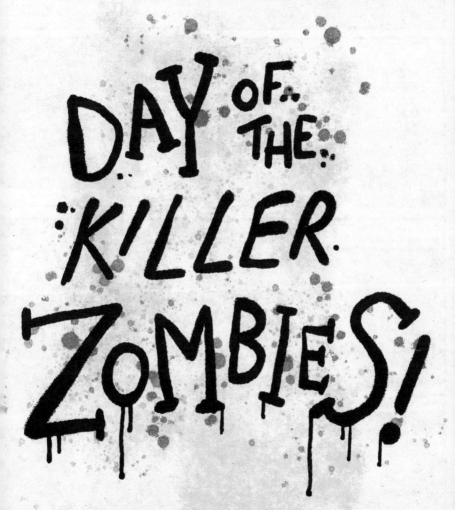

(Filmed in Eric-vision – sorry if it's a bit meh!)

IF THE RUMOURS WERE TRUE, THERE WERE ZOMBIES INSIDE...

BUT THEY WERE NO MATCH FOR...

THE LITTLE MERMAIDS!

THANKS FOR THAT TEAM NAME, COOPER.

WHAT?! IT'S CUTE!

LOCK AND LOAD, BOYS! IT'S TIME TO HUNT ZOMBIES!

THIS HARNESS THINGY IS REALLY TIGHT!

OOH! CHAFING!

WE WERE PROS, TAKING IT ALL IN, CALM, COLLECTED...

ALTHOUGH WE MAY HAVE GOT A BIT OVEREXCITED...

WOO HOO!

TIME FOR A PLAN!

STAY LOW AND TAKE SHOTS WHILE HIDDEN.

OH YEAH! BACK ON FORM!

CHAPTER TWENTY-TWO

Friday, 2.30 p.m.

Afterwards, Cooper and I sat in the cafe area of Zombie Quest having a Coke. It's nice to have refreshments after a zombie apocalypse. It was also nice imagining you being with us, Finn. In fact, it definitely felt like you were. I felt you beside me when I took those shots from up high. So weird. It was like you were telling me where to aim and what strategy to adopt next. I took a lot of your advice, but the last one – when we went all-out and dominated the zombies through chaos? Well, I'm proud to say that was all me.

Cooper was helping me finish the rough sketches of the battle when I turned to him. "Why would the zombie utter those three words at the end?" I asked.

Cooper looked up from sketching, seemingly in a world of his own. "Huh? What three words?"

And that's when it hit me.

"Of course! What Three Words!"

Cooper frowned. "Huh?"

"What Three Words! It's an app, Coops. It divides the whole world into three-metre-square sections, and each square has a unique combination of three random words which identify it. It means you can find any place on Earth with total accuracy, just by using the words!"

Cooper got busy on his phone. "I'm downloading." He smiled at me. "Good thinking!"

I smiled back. "Thanks."

"Got it. So our words are—"

"Torches, booms, crackles! It must be the next location clue from Finn!"

Cooper inputted the words and I watched as the map zeroed in on a location.

"Looks like the middle of nowhere," Cooper said, showing me his screen.

"Must be something there." I shrugged. "Even if it's

just buried treasure." I smiled. "Or Finn sitting on a log, waiting. Wouldn't that be cool?"

Cooper looked down at the table. "Let's go then."

We collected our stuff and met Aunt Caz on the way out, who was definitely flirting with one of the zombies. (Side note: I do feel she could do a bit better, like someone whose flesh isn't rotting, but I guess she's no spring chicken any more and we shouldn't judge.) We told her all about What Three Words, showed her the map, and after a lot of faffing around and explaining, and general old-person dithering, she finally understood and agreed to drive there.

We were just getting in the camper van in the car park when it hit me again. That weird feeling. *Something I should have noticed.* I looked around, but it was just a normal car park with some cars in it. I tried to think back to when I'd felt this before: outside my house, behind the football club, the high street … there was a link, I felt sure, like *déjà-vu* … something was the same, *familiar…*

"Eric? You coming?" Aunt Caz shouted, starting the engine.

I hopped inside. *Just my mind playing tricks*, I thought to myself.

A few hours later and it was starting to get dark, but after driving down a very long, very winding, very bumpy dirt track that took us right into a wood, we emerged into a small clearing.

"Torches, booms, crackles," Cooper said.

In front of us was a small log cabin. And I knew immediately what this was.

DON'T NEED TO SAY IT, — IT'S FLASHBACK TIME, BABY!!

Finn was off school for quite a long time after his diagnosis, while we all waited for the medicine to work and for him to get better. I'd often visit him at home after school, and I'd fill him in on all the gossip, tell him about what we were studying in class, and just banter and laugh in that way that you do with your best mate.

One day, I could tell Finn was feeling a bit depressed. I didn't blame him; it must've been miserable. He told me he was tired of all the doctors telling him what to do, and his parents telling him what to do, and how he just wanted to have some fun again. So I wanted to cheer him up by focusing on things we could do when he was feeling better – just stuff for me and him, no one else. I was obviously expecting Finn to come up with something huge and terrifying – like one of those space trips you can buy if you happen to have a million pounds handy. At the very least, a parachute jump.

But he didn't. He only had two things he wanted to do, and the first was to spend a night in a log cabin in the woods.

"Just you and me, no one else, and we can do whatever we like, and be whoever we like, and no one can tell us what to do because they won't be there! Wouldn't that be cool?"

I laughed. "Yeah, that sounds nice. Just me and you?"

"Just me and you." Finn nodded. "Oh, and plenty of snacks!" He offered me some Chipsticks. "Especially these. I heckin' love 'em!"

So we ate Chipsticks and kept chatting, and – skipping ahead – it was all fun until he said, "And if I don't make it, and none of that happens, then I'd want to be reincarnated."

I stared at him. "Shut up. Of course you'll make it. You're doing great."

"Know what I'd be reincarnated as?" he said, ignoring me.

"What?"

"*A seagull*. One of those aggressive ones who steal your chips at the seaside."

I laughed at that. "Why, Finn? Why be a seagull, when you could be a tiger or a … I dunno, a dolphin, or something."

He grinned at me and ruffled my hair. "Because I really like chips. I mean, I like all food, 'course I do. I love wings, and tacos, I *adore* Hawaiian pizza … but chips? Chips are king! Dolphins and tigers don't really have access to chips, Eric."

I mean, he was right about that.

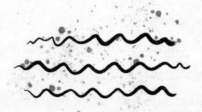

I stepped out of the camper van, and the thing that hit me was the silence. It was so peaceful. No sirens, no cars, no drilling, no talking. Just the occasional chirp of birds, but otherwise, stillness. It was so quiet, it almost made my head explode – like, my ears and brain couldn't cope with not having any noise to deal with.

The cabin sat in the middle of a clearing in the wood, the last of the sun trickling down and bathing it in a warm glow. Outside, there was a wooden hot tub and a firepit. Inside, well … it was perfect. There were sofas with blankets and extra-soft cushions, candles in lanterns, a big wooden table, doors leading off to the bedrooms and bathroom, and a small kitchen area which had the most important thing – a hamper of snacks. There was hot chocolate, with all the toppings, just like Finn would make – marshmallows, chocolate to grate on top and Mars bars. There was also bread, eggs, cheese, bottles of fresh juice, and, of course, a big bag of salt and vinegar Chipsticks.

A tear trickled down my cheek. Finn's favourite. He "heckin' loved 'em". I quickly wiped the tear away and turned to Cooper and Aunt Caz. "Cool, huh?"

"There's no TV," Cooper said, "but there's a stack of board games – including Hungry Hippos, a personal favourite – and a really nice chessboard!"

I looked at the chessboard. Heavy looking, ornately carved wooden pieces on a marble board atop a chunky wooden pedestal. "Nice! Can you play, Coops?"

Cooper nodded. "I mean, I wouldn't call myself 'good', but I know how they all move."

"Don't do yourself down," I told him. "We'll play later. I bet you're better than you think."

"There's a weird old-fashioned phone too," Cooper said, pointing at the contraption sitting on a table near the door. "Just as well, since there's zero mobile reception here."

"Total solitude," I muttered. "No one to bother us. No one to say anything. Just you and me, Finn." I took a deep breath, then looked at Cooper and Aunt Caz. "Sorry. It's just, we always said we'd do something like this."

"Aw, that's nice," Aunt Caz said. "Finn was a thoughtful boy."

I nodded. "Wish he was here."

"Me too," said Cooper.

Aunt Caz clapped her hands together. "All right, how about we sort some food out?"

"Finn would approve of that," I said.

"Find me a twelve-year-old boy who wouldn't!" Aunt Caz laughed.

We unpacked the hamper, and while there were certainly food options, it had been a long day, and while we were all quite peckish, none of us could really be bothered to cook. Which is when we found the leaflet, nestling in the bottom of the food hamper.

FINN'S PIZZERIA

The finest pizzas, delivered to your door!

Everything is topped with pineapple – *deal with it!*
We only accept orders from boys called Eric.

Call us!

(If you're called Eric, and a boy.)

901-101-453

"That's a weird phone number for the UK," Cooper said.

"It's a weird note," I replied. I glanced over at the old-fashioned phone sitting on the table by the door. "I guess I call then, do I?"

"I don't think this is for real pizza," Cooper said. "This is a clue."

I smiled, because that much was surely obvious. "Oh, you think?"

"Shame, because I would really like some pizza right now."

I walked over to the phone and poked about.

"But if it turns out I'm wrong, and it is pizza, I'll have a meat feast," Cooper continued.

"I'll have anything vegetarian," Aunt Caz said. "Maybe they've got butternut squash and feta cheese?"

"OK, just to say it again, I don't think we're gonna be getting any pizza out of this. Finn's amazing, he's capable of great things, but I don't think he's running a pizza restaurant in the vicinity." I frowned at the phone. "Is this like a mobile thing? It isn't even plugged in."

It was certainly unusual. We had a landline phone at home, but it was very much plugged in to a socket in the wall. No one ever used it.

"Dial the number and see what happens?" Aunt Caz suggested.

I looked at the phone. "But how? There are no buttons!"

Aunt Caz explained that you have to put your finger into the hole with the first number you want to dial, and then you rotate the dial around until it stops, then let it go, then do the same with the second number, and so on.

I mean, seriously?! Who invented this ridiculous contraption?

Anyway, holding the heavy and cumbersome handset in one hand, I dialled with the other. There were a series of clicks. Silence. And then...

"Hey, Eric? Is that you?"

"Finn? No way! Is it? FINN!"

CHAPTER TWENTY-THREE

Friday, 8.30 p.m.

My hands were shaking, my whole body was shaking, tears streamed down my face. I was right about him being alive! Take that, you doubters!

It was Finn. He was here. Well, not here, but he was somewhere, and he was talking. Finally! All I wanted. I was right. I'd always been right. No one else believed, but I did.

"Finn! Oh god, thank you," I croaked.

"This is what we always dreamed of, huh?" Finn said.

"Yeah," I muttered.

"Do me a favour," he said. "Pick the phone up – you

may have noticed it isn't plugged in – and go outside."

"Huh, OK, sure…" I picked it up and headed out the door, ignoring the questioning looks of Coops and Aunt Caz. "Oh, Finn – where are you? Where have you bee—"

"You outside yet?"

"Um, yeah. I'm outside."

There was a pause.

"Finn?" I said.

"See the firepit in the middle?"

"Yeah."

"Head there, and just to the side of it lie on the grass on your back."

I walked over and lay down by the pit, staring up at the night sky, the phone handset pressed to my ear. "OK, I'm here…"

I waited. More silence.

"You there?"

"I'm here! Finn, it's so good to talk to—"

"Look up, Eric. I'm hoping you can see the stars. Can you see the stars?"

"Yeah, stars," I croaked, my voice shaking. I couldn't

believe it was finally him. "Lots of stars. Where are you, Finn?"

"Lots of stars, huh?"

"Yeah, I just said. Loads."

"Never seen so many, have you?"

"I guess not. But, Finn, never mind the stars, I—"

"So I came here, Eric. I came to this place and spent two nights here. Wanted to check it out, check it was just right. It kinda made me sad, 'cause it felt like we should be doing it together, like we said we would."

"Yeah—"

"And then I came out here, and I lay down where you're pretty much lying now, and I looked up at the stars, and ... well, I know this sounds super cheesy, but it made me happy again, because I was looking at the same stars I knew you would be looking at. So, in a weird way, this was something we could experience together – maybe not at exactly the same time, but still together, kind of..."

I was crying. "But I want you here with me, Finn ... please, just—"

"As long as it isn't cloudy, of course! That would mess

all this up! It's not cloudy, is it, Eric?"

"No. I can see the stars."

"Eric, you're near the end of the adventure I planned now. Everything will make sense soon. You'll find out what it's all been about. I promise."

"Promise?"

"Now … you need to reread all my notes so far. Carefully. There's something you've missed. Check the small print. And then … *your move*, I think."

"What? I don't—"

"Love you, matey. Remember that."

"I love you too, Finn. Finn! Please, I know—"

"Over and out!"

I was sobbing, but I managed to choke out, "Roger that!"

There were a few more clicks, then the line went dead.

And I sobbed and sobbed and sobbed and sobbed and—

"Eric?" It was Cooper. He kneeled down beside me and wrapped his arms around me. "Come on, dude. It's OK. It's OK."

"It was Finn!" I spluttered.

"Yeah, I gathered."

"Quick!" I said. "We need to call back!"

With shaking hands, I dialled the number on the pizza leaflet again. I waited, then heard the familiar series of clicks.

"Hey, Eric? Is that you?"

"Yes! It's me again! Finn, for god's sake—"

"This is what we always dreamed of, huh?"

"Yes, I know, you said that before and—"

"Do me a favour... Pick the phone up – you may have noticed it isn't plugged in – and go outside."

My hand went limp, the receiver dropping down by my side. Yes, it was Finn's voice, but it was pre-recorded. I had thought he was speaking to me for real, but it was just a message.

"You outside yet?"

I let the handset fall to the ground. Cooper put his arm around my shoulders again, while I felt all the hope drain out of me. "I thought he was really there," I muttered.

"I guess, maybe sometimes, when we really, really

want something to be true, we can make ourselves believe it is. Even when … even when there's no way it can be."

I couldn't stop crying. And when I looked at Coops, he was crying too.

"Hey, um…" Cooper sniffed and cleared his throat. "Sometimes … when my nan passed away, one thing we did was share things we remembered about her, and it kinda helped a bit. It was nice."

"Finn's not dead, Coops."

"Sure… But he's not here, is he? And … I guess I never knew him that well, and it'd be good to know more. So … got any stories?"

"I dunno."

"Like … do you have a favourite Finn memory? Something he did … that was funny, or nice, or just … *Finn-Fabulous?*"

I chuckled. *"Finn-Fabulous!* I like that!" I glanced at Coops. "Yeah, actually, there is one thing."

Cooper started waving his arms about. "Shall we?"

"Flashback! Yeah!"

"Me and Finn had this big row. We'd had rows before – I guess everyone does from time to time – but this one was … epic. Epically bad, I mean. I said stuff I shouldn't have said … stuff I didn't mean, and Finn did too, and I guess we … well, it doesn't matter. The point is, it was bad. And I felt like I couldn't forgive Finn. *Ever.*"

"What was the row about?" Cooper asked.

"I don't want to talk about it. Anyway, the next day I was moping around school. I was this weird mix of angry, sad, frustrated, hurt… I just felt kind of raw about it all. Finn was off school because he was obviously poorly, and that was probably a good thing right then because I didn't want to have to speak to him anyway. That lunchtime, I walked into the cafeteria, ready to eat my lunch alone, and there's Finn, sitting at our usual table, and he's only gone and set it up like a posh restaurant. He's put a starched white tablecloth on the table, silver cutlery, there are plates, some actual wine glasses that he's filled with juice, a little vase of flowers in the middle, and even a candle. There are two plates of food too, one for him, and, I guess, one for me. He wasn't even meant to be in school. He was too sick to come in, but he'd dragged himself there, because … he wanted to say sorry, I suppose."

Cooper nodded. "Yeah, I remember, because—"

"Right?" I chuckled. "It was amazing. And Finn … he glanced up, and he saw me, and he … gave me this big, beautiful, hopeful smile, like 'Hey, it's OK, doofus!' type of smile. And I…" I swallowed again, my throat tight at the memory and all my shame. "And … everyone was looking, and it was so much, and I wasn't expecting it, and I was scared… Scared of what we might say to each other, and what people might say about us, because this was … a bit unusual, right? Boys don't … have candlelit lunches together. It's… So I…" More tears started flowing down my cheeks. "I walked out of the cafeteria, Cooper. I turned my back on him and I walked out."

"Oh, Eric." Cooper hugged me tight, but it didn't help,

because it wasn't a hug from him I wanted right then.

"I turned my back on him. Because I was scared. And I let him sit there, having done all that, eating his lunch by himself with everyone staring. Because I'm a coward. And the thing is, I really, really wanted to go and sit with him. It was the nicest, most wonderful thing that anyone has ever done for me. But I didn't. And soon after that his parents took him away on that big holiday, and when he came back ... he was even sicker, and ... so I never got to say... I never got to say I was sorry. About the lunch, about the row before that. Any of it. And that can't be, because me and Finn ... we're best mates, and we'll always be best mates, and it can't end with us not being... And when I think back, he did all that, and he must have been feeling so ill, but he did it anyway, he did all that, for me. For us. So I missed my chance, Cooper. I missed my chance because I'm just a useless, scared coward." I swallowed. "And that's my favourite memory of Finn, because it reminds me that he's a much better person than I am."

"You're not—"

"No, it's fine, it's just something for me to aspire to.

He's my hero, Cooper. We all need our heroes, and I sure as hell need mine."

I waved my arms about. "End of flashback."

"Eric?" Cooper murmured after a bit. "Just so you know … Finn didn't end up sitting all alone." He met my eyes and sighed. "Because I sat there."

"Huh?"

"The cafeteria was full, Eric. There were literally no seats left, except the one opposite Finn. So I asked if I could sit there."

"And he agreed?"

"He said, 'As long as you don't mind everyone staring at us and this ridiculous over-the-top table set-up!' And I replied, 'Hey, you're looking at someone who submitted an assignment in *binary code* and has a *Keep Calm and Do Some Science* T-shirt – do you think I care what anyone thinks?!' He laughed at that, and we chatted, and I'd never really spoken with Finn before, but he seemed really cool." Cooper swallowed. "Anyway, just so you know, he wasn't alone. And he seemed OK, Eric. He seemed like he understood why you weren't there."

I turned to Cooper and smiled. "So that's why he picked you for this. Because you don't care what people think, and I always do, and so we balance each other out, like me and Finn do. Now I get it!"

Cooper chuckled. "Never thought of it like that. Guess it makes sense?"

"Thanks for telling me that, Coops," I muttered.

We sat in silence for a bit, under the same stars that Finn loved so much. "What do you want to do now?" Cooper asked.

"I think we should eat … and then we carry on. Finn's message said there's something we missed. We need to get all the notes out and take another look."

We went back inside the cabin, where Aunt Caz was making omelettes. "I'm guessing the pizza delivery didn't work out?" she said.

"Something like that," I replied.

Cooper and I sat down at the big table, and I unfolded all the notes and laid them out in front of us. "Look at the small print," Finn had said. "Something we've missed."

So we did...

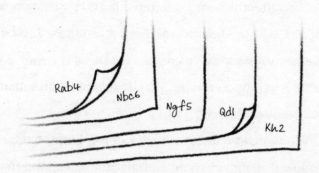

I focused in on the tiny writing. *"Your move,"* I muttered, remembering Finn's words. It clicked, and I snapped my head up, looking at the chessboard in the corner. "This is chess notation!" I exclaimed. "Finn made us join chess club at the start of Year 7 – he wanted us to try new things. Each of these codes corresponds to a move in chess! He wants us to place the pieces in particular spots on the board!"

I bounded over to the chess set, Cooper hot on my heels. "OK," I said, rubbing my hands together. "He said *your move*, and since no one has yet moved on this board, and it's my move first, we need to move the white pieces, as they always go first."

Cooper nodded, hanging on my every word.

"Imagine the board is lettered left to right from 'a' to 'h'. OK? And downwards, from 8 to 1. So – Rab4. R means rook. But we've got two rooks, so the rook we move is sitting on square 'a', and we move it to square b4." I moved the rook. "Got it?"

We worked through, moving each piece, Cooper reading out the notation, and me translating it into a move on the board. King to h2 was the last move, and I placed the piece down with a satisfying clunk.

There was a whirring sound, and a secret drawer popped open in the base!

I snapped my fingers. "Bingo!" I grinned. "What's inside?"

Cooper pulled out some slips of card and held them up. "Train tickets. Looks like we're heading to Penzance. First class."

CHAPTER TWENTY-FOUR

Saturday, 8 a.m.

"Charmed, I'm sure!" I said, sweeping my feather boa back around my shoulders as I nodded to the customer service host and boarded the train at London Paddington – first class! I had never travelled first class before, so I wasn't entirely sure how to dress and behave, but it was clearly very posh, so I was confident I was on the right track.

"Charmed, I'm sure!" Cooper added, absolutely rocking his tweed suit, complete with pocket watch and peaked cap. "I'll take the salmon en croûte, and my friend will have the steak – medium rare."

"The restaurant car opens after we've left

Paddington," the bemused customer host replied.

"Charmed, I'm sure!" I said.

Of course, it soon became abundantly clear that we were dressed all wrong, looked like a right pair of dorks, and not a single other soul was saying "Charmed, I'm sure!" or, indeed, any variation of it. To be fair, Aunt Caz had tried to tell us this, which was why she was sitting at the opposite end of the carriage, pretending that she didn't know us. And, to be even fairer, I did kind of know really, but do you know what? I didn't care. This was fun. Coops and I were having a laugh – and why not? It's not every day you get to travel first class, it's not every day you have to leave at four in the morning for the drive down to London and are hysterical with tiredness, and it's not every day you know for sure you're on the final leg of a quest and will be reunited with your long-lost friend very soon.

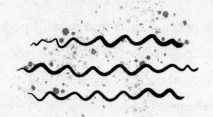

"OK, Finn, when you're better – which will be *so* soon – you want to stay in a log cabin in the woods. But what was the second thing you wanted to do?" I asked.

Finn smiled. "Ever been to Cornwall, Eric?"

"I have not."

"We'll go there. It's beautiful. And we'll get chips, and we'll sit on the wall by the beach, and eat them while looking out over the sea." He winked at me. "You know how much I love chips. Which reminds me, if I don't make it, and I'm reincarnated..."

DOO-WOP-DA-DO-DO

"Ooh, that's the mobile!"

"You should change the ringtone," Cooper sniffed,

perusing the lunch menu card on the table.

"Finn set it. Whatever Finn wants." I swiped at the notification. "It's a voice memo!"

"Hey, Eric. If you are hearing this, that means you're finally on the train heading to Cornwall. Make sure you take full advantage of the first-class tickets. Did you know you can have pretty much anything you like, food and drink-wise, and it's all FREE? When you arrive in Penzance, there's a chip shop on Western Promenade Road. Go there and say you're collecting Finn's order, then head to the beach and find a nice spot. Over and out, buddy."

"Roger that! How can he possibly know we're on the train? How is he watching all this?" I muttered. I glanced at Cooper, wondering if he had any kind of opinion on this, but he was engrossed in his own phone. "Coops?"

"Is it good or bad your mum is sharing your photo on Facebook?"

I squeezed my eyes shut. "Show me..." I glanced at his phone. "Oh god, there's a hashtag and everything – #FindEric – ahhhh! Why is she like this?! Why can't she be like your mum and just be chill? I'm gonna have to call her." I blew out a breath and dialled Mum.

"*Eric?!*"

"Mum, hi, I'm sorry, it's me, I'm fine, you can … call off the search."

"It's *not* fine! Caz said you were going to meditation camp – *where are you?*"

"I'm fine, that's all that matters!"

"Eric Griffin, I swear to god, you are going to tell me exactly where you are, I am coming to get you, and you are grounded for the rest of the year. I have been in such a state! You're not old enough to just do whatever you like. There are *criminals* out there, Eric! Bad people! Danger!"

I mean, sure, that was true. But there was also fun and adventure and, you know, *good times.*

"Mum, you need to chill."

"Tell me where you are, else I'm going to the police."

I sighed, knowing it was no good. "Cornwall. *Penzance.*"

The phone went dead as we suddenly went through a tunnel, but maybe that was for the best. I felt like all of Finn's plans were about to be ruined. I pulled the feather boa off and slumped down in my seat. "Why does my mum want to ruin everything?" I crossed my arms and slumped down further. Mum, who always told me not to do things. Mum, who talked about risk and failure, but never fun. Mum, who was all about controlling me, every second of every day – and for what? To make me miserable? I bet the last thing she wanted was for me to find Finn. I bet she hated him. Finn always wanted me to take the leap into the unknown and do stuff just for the hell of it.

I bet Mum's glad he's gone.

And then I froze.

What was I even thinking?

Glad he's gone?

Gone?

But … Finn hasn't gone.

I don't know why that idea even came into my head.

I put my earbuds in and lost myself in a Spotify playlist. I thought it was best I didn't do any more thinking right then.

Several hours, a very tasty free fish pie, ten free bags of crisps, eight free mini cakes, twelve free packs of biscuits, and a lot of free Coke and water later, we pulled in to Penzance.

I stretched as I stepped out into the crisp Cornish air. Nice as first class was, I was glad we'd finally arrived. Around me, swarms of people, probably on their holidays, dragged huge suitcases behind them as they made their way towards the exit, talking about "surf" and "golfing" and "boat trips". I felt weird. Almost a bit ... sorry for myself. I think I wanted to be on a fun holiday too. And yet, I was there to find Finn – so why did I feel so ... on edge?

Maybe it was some kind of sixth sense, because as the crowds started to clear ahead of us, I saw three police officers waiting. I froze. *What had Mum done?* My mouth was dry. I looked around me – where was Cooper? And then...

They started walking towards me.

I backed away, but Aunt Caz bumped into me. "Eric?" she said. And then she saw them coming over. "Oh no."

I turned – still no Cooper! – and started walking quickly away, but—

A strong, uniformed arm grabbed hold of me. "Not so fast, little guy!"

And, honestly, I don't know what's more humiliating – being arrested at a train station in front of a huge crowd, or being twelve and referred to as "little guy".

Having reflected on it, I think it's the latter.

CHAPTER TWENTY-FIVE

Saturday, 2 p.m.

I was expecting to be strip-searched, handcuffed and thrown in a cell, but they put me in a room with a sofa, pot plants and cuddly toys. The door was unlocked, they brought me drinks and snacks, and everyone was really nice.

If anything, that was worse.

It was like … they pitied me.

I got the sense Aunt Caz was possibly in a bit more trouble, however, since they talked to her separately, and there were raised voices, and I heard Aunt Caz say things like "hysterical" and "blown out of proportion" and "let me tell you, my sister is an absolute nightmare!".

When Aunt Caz came back in, she was very red-faced and told me she should "never have got involved with all this".

"Why did you then?" I asked.

"Finn asked me!" she said. "How could I say no?"

"Because he was dying?"

"Yes, Eric. Exactly." She sighed. And then her brow furrowed, and she looked frantically around the room. "Where's Cooper?!"

I shrugged. "How should I know? I was bundled into a police van! I thought he was with you."

Aunt Caz's eyes widened. And then she swore. And then she ran out of the room.

I think it's probably for the best that Aunt Caz doesn't have kids herself. Not being rude, but I happen to know that she didn't even manage to keep her goldfish alive a couple of years ago, so I just don't think she's cut out for it.

I sighed and looked at the stained carpet. Mum was on her way down to collect me. All I'd wanted was to find Finn. That's all. I would have given anything to give him a hug, see his face, and laugh with him again. Finn wanted me to complete this quest, but how could I now? He never factored in a prison break. And anyway … maybe it didn't matter any more. Maybe everyone was right. Maybe I was just kidding myself. Maybe…

Tears sprang from my eyes again. *Jeez, Eric, you have done so much crying recently!* I don't know if that's ever gonna stop, to be honest. But maybe that doesn't matter either. They're tears for you, Finn. For everything that should have been, and everything that never will be now.

And then the mobile chirped.

> You need to get out of there. Is anyone with you?

Finn was texting me again!

> I'm alone.

> Is door unlocked?

> Yes.

> Walk out. Ask to go to toilet. Wait by door. You will hear a commotion. That's your cue. Leave toilet, walk out of exit. Keep phone in your hands for instructions. Go NOW.

My heart leapt into my throat. I didn't give myself time to think. I had to just do it. As casually as I could, I swung the door open and walked out into the main reception area.

"Can I go to the toilet?" I asked the policeman behind the desk, adding a pointless little jig to aid my case.

"'Course!" He waved me in the direction of the gents.

I nipped in and waited behind the door. The phone bleeped.

> Stand by.

I held my breath.

Swallowed.

Fidgeted a bit.

Looked at my phone again.

And then…

There was some sort of low-level moan outside the door, followed by the promised "commotion".

I inched the door ajar. In reception, an elderly lady was lying on the floor, looking like she'd fainted … and looking slightly familiar, if I'm honest, but that didn't matter right then. With two policemen tending to her, the coast was clear. I slipped out, stalked across the reception and went straight out the main door, taking an immediate left turn, just like I was told.

Oh wow, Finn must have been watching me, because how else could he know? I took the left. And I stopped dead because I realized what it was that had been making me feel weird all those times. Parked in the road was a little yellow MINI. And I realized that same MINI had been parked on my street when I was digging up the boxes, and parked behind the football club ... on the high street ... at the Zombie Quest place...

ROUND TO THE RIGHT, STAY ON PENALVERNE PLACE

I didn't have time to think about that any more. This was completely wild and I just had to go with it. I looked over my shoulder. No police were on my tail, and no one else appeared to be watching me. How was this even happening?

MOVE, ERIC! MOVE!

I sprinted off; the messages kept coming – left, along, right, another left, down an alley, right, take the left fork ... eventually I came out into a park, limping because something was in my shoe. Some kind of pebble, I guessed. I was pretty sure I'd escaped for now, so I hobbled to the grass, flopped down and pulled my trainer off.

"What the heck?"

I pulled the device out from where it was wedged under the inner sole of the trainer that Finn had given me. It must have come loose with all the running. I knew what this was.

A tracking device!

What?! Why?! How?!

"Stick your hands in the air!"

Oh god! I did what I was told and kneeled on the ground for good measure, like I'd seen in films. "I come in peace!" I said, although I wasn't sure that was quite the right response.

Someone started hooting with laugher. I looked up.

Cooper.

"Ah, man! Your face!" He giggled. He put on a squeaky voice. "I come in peace! Hahaha!"

"OK, first, my voice isn't that high, it's totally breaking ... or will be, at some point soon; second, where have you been, and third, what are you doing here and were those messages from you?"

"Eric, I just made a swift and efficient exit at the train station when I saw the feds. I figured you'd be at the police station, so I made my way over and waited … until I saw you run out and I followed. What's going on?"

"Coops, I have no idea, except … these trainers Finn gave me? They had a tracking device in them!"

"Ohhhhh," Cooper said. "So that's how!"

"How what?"

"Well, *someone* knew where we were the whole time, right? And we weren't being followed … except by that yellow MINI. You knew that, right?"

"Yeah, I … figured that out a while ago. Just didn't say."

"Question is – who's behind all this?"

At that point the yellow MINI pulled up at the edge of the park and tooted its horn.

"Guess we're about to find out the truth," I said. I took a deep breath. A big part of me didn't want to find out, because the truth didn't feel like something I wanted to face right then. The truth felt like it would be final. But I guess you can't hide from the truth forever. So, scared and trembling, I put one foot in front of the other, and I walked towards the car. Towards the truth.

CHAPTER TWENTY-SIX

Saturday, 4 p.m.

Well, I was right about one thing.

Finn's gran was involved.

Just not in the way I thought she was.

Cooper and I sat in the back of Finn's grandparents' MINI as they explained everything to us.

"This was something Finn wanted to do for you," his gran told me. "He and I spent many hours talking about it when he was too unwell to get out of bed … many times you nearly caught us, walking in just as we were scheming and plotting."

"Why would he do that when he was sick?"

"Finn loved nothing more than a prank," his granddad said. "You know that, Eric. He loved tricks and cons, and riddles and puzzles. He got an awful lot of pleasure from setting this up for you."

"But when did he set it all up?"

"His parents took him on that amazing holiday, remember?" his gran said.

"Yeah?"

"Well, he did that, and then he spent a week with me, and we toured all over the country, putting everything in place. We made sure the hairdressing salon had your appointment booked, got your football shirt printed, the photos were sent to Snappy Snaps, that the zombie was ready to meet you at the bottom of the zip wire and the cabin in the woods was all set up. We also buried the boxes in your garden, and I had to get the code for your shed out of your mother!"

"How did you do that?"

"I told her I wanted to hide a present for Finn in there – a metal detector. I simply watched as she entered the code for the padlock. Then, when you were at school, I came round with Finn so we could talk to your mum about how Finn's illness wasn't looking so good, and how to help you deal with that. When Finn popped to the loo, he hid the code in your mum's Christmas cupboard!"

"That is some operation!" I said.

"Oh, and that's just the start of it. This whole adventure was so finely tuned – you had to turn up at the log cabin exactly when we'd booked it for, for example, so from the moment I sent you the fake invite to the funeral, telling you to dress as a unicorn, everything had to run like clockwork. Of course, me and Wilf were able to track you via your trainers, but we also needed to follow you and make sure you were solving the clues correctly. You might recall the old lady under the dryer at the hairdresser—"

"The donkey mascot at football?" Finn's granddad interjected.

"That was you two?!" I howled.

"The clipboard survey woman on the high street?"

"No way!"

"I was pretty confident you wouldn't get too close to her!" Finn's gran laughed. "And then Wilf was one of the zombies too!"

"Torches, booms, crackles!" his granddad croaked.

"Good, huh? You never suspected, did you? Not under all that make-up!"

"And, of course, I was the old lady who collapsed in the police station just now. What we and Finn didn't fully account for was your mother, Eric."

"Speaking of which..." Coops said, looking out of the window.

There, walking across the park, was my mum. I sighed. "I'd better go and speak to her." I looked at Finn's grandparents. "This isn't over."

"Oh, I know!" his gran said, smiling. "You've the finale to come yet!"

I climbed out of the car to intercept my mum. "I'm sorry," I said, getting in there first. "I'll reflect on what I've done."

"Eric, I was so worried—"

"I know, I—"

"I don't want to ever lose you!"

"Mum, I know, I—"

"You *don't* know," she said.

She sat down on a bench, playing with her locket between her fingers.

I sat down next to her. "Mum?"

She opened the locket. "Do you know who this is, Eric?"

"Yeah. It's me. As a baby."

She shook her head. "No. It's your big brother."

"But ... I don't have a big brother. I'm an only child."

"No, Eric, you do. Or rather, you did. Three years before you were born, I had a little boy. His name was Ernie. He was born prematurely, and he was doing OK ... they kept him in hospital, and days went by, and it was fine. I only popped home to get some sleep for a few hours, but he ... while I was away ... he died, Eric. He just ... passed away. And I wasn't there. And I always wonder ... if I had been, might things have been different? Could I have alerted the doctors sooner..." She shook her head slowly. "I still feel guilty, even now."

I stared at her, trying to take it all in. I had a brother? Why didn't anyone tell me? It was like Mum had been pretending it never happened. I reached out and took her hand. "It's not your fault, Mum."

"Ever since, I suppose I've been afraid ... that if I'm not there, if I don't know what you're doing and when ...

253

then it could happen again." She smiled sadly. "But that's no way to live, is it? Afraid. Not doing things." She glanced towards the MINI. "I saw Caz outside the police station. She filled me in on everything. Life's short, isn't it? Shorter than you think it's going to be sometimes."

I swallowed. "Why didn't you tell me?"

"I didn't want to burden you with it, Eric. Thinking about him makes me so sad – I didn't want you to be sad too. Sometimes it's easier just to shut it all away."

I understood what that felt like.

And I understood then what I'd been doing too.

Shutting the truth away because it was too painful to deal with.

I looked back towards the car, and to where Cooper was watching me out of the window. "I think ... talking helps though, sometimes?"

"You're right. It does."

"So. *Ernie*. Sounds like we would have been a right double act."

Mum smiled. "Yeah."

We sat in silence for a bit while I thought about the big brother I never knew and about how Mum felt, about the guilt, and how that was something I felt too with how I'd left things with Finn after our big row. What if he didn't know I was sorry? What if he'd died thinking I hated him? I didn't hate him. Of course I didn't, but I never told him that and now ... it was too late.

"Can I tell you something about Finn? Something that happened between us?"

Mum nodded.

"OK, so..." I waved my arms about. "That means flashback, OK?"

Mum smiled and nodded again.

Me and Finn had had a massive row. Worse than ever. I'd gone round to see him one afternoon after school. He was looking pretty good, actually. Less tired, more energy. Eyes sparkling, like they always did. And then he dropped this bombshell:

"Eric, just so you know, we've decided to stop the treatment."

"What? Why?" I spluttered. "Are you better?"

He shook his head. "Nah. It's just not working any more, and it makes me feel so bad, it'll be nicer if I don't carry it on."

"But … if you're not better, then what'll happen?"

Finn looked me right in the eyes. He couldn't say it. But I knew.

"No, Finn, no!" I said, panic rising. "You *have* to!"

"Eric, ever since I got sick, everyone has been telling me what I have to do. Go for this test, take bloods, have this injection, that injection, go for a scan … but now … there's nothing more they can do, so—"

"There's always something!" I shouted. "There has to be! That doctor in Mexico! There are cures! Why would you just give up?" And then I added, "What about me?!"

And Finn said, "This isn't about you."

And I told him *it was*, because we'd promised, years ago, that we were in this together, we were a team, we'd face the world, come what may, and now he was just giving up, and I told him he was "selfish" and a "bad friend", and he said I wasn't being a good friend right then either, and that I can't just try to control him and what he does like I do everything, and I was like, "What the hell does *that* mean?" and he said, "Life sometimes just happens and there's nothing you can do and you shouldn't try," and I told him that was pathetic, that was giving up, and I was disappointed in him ... but I didn't mean it. I was upset, and I was angry, because I didn't want Finn taken away from me, because I'd planned for us to be *forever*, and I couldn't believe ... how could he die? How's that possible? How's that fair?! Just ... *no*.

"You're disappointed in me?" Finn said, glaring at me. "After everything I've been through? After the absolute hell I've been through, all the pain and sickness, not doing anything I love, stuck here, *sick*, and you're disappointed in me?" He shook his head. "*Wow*. Well, I'm sorry not to live up to your expectations, Eric!"

"I just meant..."

"I know what you meant!" Finn snapped. "You were

thinking of yourself. Wondering how you'd get by without me by your side. Well, I guess you'll have to learn to stand up for yourself, Eric. You'll have to learn to fight your own battles. But it's good to know that's all I am to you – someone you can use to make your life easier!"

"Finn, I don't think—"

"Yeah, you do."

"Well, what am I to you then?" I said, blinking back tears.

Finn shrugged. "You're no one, Eric. No one."

"Yeah?" I screamed. "Well, you're no one to me too! I wish I'd never even met you!"

I stormed out that afternoon. I didn't know what to say and everything *he* had said was a massive shock.

He tried to make things better the next day. He even came into school. But I wasn't ready. I was still angry with him.

And then he went on his trip.

And I know now, during that time away, or at least for part of it, he set up this adventure for me.

Because I wasn't "no one" to him.

Because he loved me.

Because he was my friend.

Even after I'd been mean to him.

I eventually wrote him a note, saying how sorry I was, but I figured it would be better if I told him myself.

But when I finally saw him again, when he got back, he was too sick, and I never got to say...

I didn't mean it, Finn.

I'm sorry, Finn.

I love you, Finn.

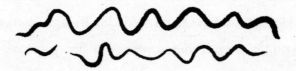

When I'd finished, Mum wrapped me in her arms while I sobbed.

"I think you just told him, Eric."

"But he doesn't know! He can't hear me!" I blubbed.

"Eric, sweetheart, when you're scared, sometimes it feels easier to shut yourself off from everything, because that way it seems like you won't get hurt so badly. Like being in a haunted house, and curling up in the corner hoping the ghosts won't find you. That's what your argument with Finn was about – pretending you meant nothing to each other because if that was true, if neither of you cared, what would there be to be sad about? Finn knew that too, I'm sure. And he wouldn't have done all this if he hadn't forgiven you. You knew each other better than anyone, right?"

I sniffed and wiped my eyes. "Yeah."

"Then he knew you were sorry. And this was his way of telling you he was sorry too, and that, actually, you meant the world to him. Trust me."

"I still wish I'd actually told him, though. You gotta do things, even if they scare you, when you have the chance, right?"

"I think that's probably right," Mum said.

That's the thing I've learned from all this. You've just got to be brave ... get the wild haircut, hang out with people you think you've nothing in common with and give them a chance, eat the Christmas food, jump into the unknown and fly down the zip wire, fight the zombies, lead a team, save the world, but also know when to kick back, relax and just let life drift on by, enjoy the silence and look at the stars. Tell people what they mean to you. Tell them you love them. Just be brave and do it.

I see that now.

I thought I was going on this adventure to find Finn.

But that was never what he planned.

He had a much bigger gift in mind.

He wanted me to find myself.

And, in that moment, I did.

CHAPTER TWENTY-SEVEN

Saturday, 5 p.m.

I wasn't the least bit hungry, but we went to the chip shop, just like Finn had instructed, and picked up the order.

Cod and chips for me and Cooper. The man behind the counter handed me the wrapped packages and I was just about to leave, but ... it didn't feel right.

"Can I have chips and barbecue chicken wings too, please?" I asked.

I didn't do it because I thought he would meet us at the seafront, I did it to honour him.

The man smiled, shovelled some more chips on to a fresh piece of paper, planted some chicken wings on top, wrapped it and handed it to me.

"On the house," he told me.

"Really? I've got money—"

"For Finn, right?" He smiled.

"Yeah. For Finn," I said. My heart swelled a bit. The fact other people spoke of Finn so warmly felt good.

The seafront was only a short walk. We sat on a stone wall overlooking the beach and the vast ocean that stretched out in front of us. It was beautiful. Breathtaking. I wished Finn was here to see it, like we always planned. I won't ever stop missing him, and I won't ever stop being sad about it, but Finn's shown me how to live, he's shown me I can, and I owe it to him to be my best self and make him proud.

I unwrapped my chips, because, at the end of the day, they were chips. It would be one hundred per cent rude not to.

On the paper inside, a web address was scribbled.

I looked at Cooper.

"On it," he said, already tapping it into his phone. "Huh. Looks like an audio file."

"Press play," I said.

Hey, buddy! If you're listening to this, it means you made it. You did it and I'm proud of you! As I'm sure you've realized by now (because you're a bright boy, Eric!), I wanted you to see how fun life can be when it isn't always planned. Sometimes the best stuff happens when you least expect it. The unknown is scary – boy, do I know that, as I sit here, not sure what's next for me in a few weeks' or months' time – but sometimes you've just got to embrace that, throw your head back, laugh at the world, and shout, "Whatever you've got for me, bring it on!"

I know you were scared of the unknown too, Eric. And I hope you can see now that you don't need to be. Be brave. Have courage. Do your own thing, even if no one else is doing it. Nothing good ever came of following the crowd. Live your life, not someone else's. Who cares what other people think? Embrace the unexpected – I'm convinced that's where the real living happens, Eric. And that's what I want you to do. Stop being sad and get busy living. Oh, and whatever you do ... do it big, do it right, and do it with style!

In completing this challenge, you've proved you

don't need me. Eric, that's been the thing I've been worrying about the most. And I know that scared you too. We always talked about how we would take on the world together, and that *was* totally my plan, but it seems my useless body had other ideas. I hate the idea of leaving you and I need to know you're gonna be OK. Doing this proves you will be. And, in case you didn't know, you have so many people who love you and will be there for you. Just look at everyone who has been involved in this crazy little caper I set up! And just so you know, the football lads will always invite you for pizza, and I hope you've seen that Cooper is an amazing, loyal and very kind person and I want you to know I fully approve of you two being best buds, since I'm no longer around.

Although I'm still your best bud too, of course. And I always will be. Because I'll be around forever. See, I found the secret of immortality, Eric. That bit was true. You've probably got it in your rucksack right now. The diary I asked you to keep? If you write about someone, even if you just *talk* about someone, then you keep their memory alive. That's what I want you to do, Eric. Write up this last adventure we had as the most amazing thing ever. Give it a great title — preferably using my name! Make sure it has a really obscure quote at the beginning that everyone thinks is really deep but is actually just nonsense. Find a world-class illustrator to draw the pictures — we both know you can't really draw, and, if necessary, get some author guy — maybe that funny one who came to our school that time to talk about the boy with bad luck — to correct your grammar and make it read a bit better. Get it published, Eric! I just want the world to know. I want the world to know that … Finn Jones was here. That I was part of this. That I existed. That I laughed, and joked, and I played pranks, I did things, I went places, I did schoolwork, I was a gamer, I enjoyed food, I watched too much YouTube … and that I loved.

I loved you, Eric.

And, about our fight? Eric, I never really got to say how sorry I was. I said stuff I obviously didn't mean. And I know you did too. I'm sorry. And I know you're sorry. Don't you dare let any of that eat you up. Forget about it. Doesn't matter. I know what you're like – you'll overthink it and get sad. Don't you *dare* get sad, Eric. Else I'll haunt you. You don't want that – because you know I'll be the super scary type of ghost that makes you pee yourself!

So, this is it, my friend. The end of our adventure. And you will go on and have many more, and me … well, not so much. I'm sorry about that, for me and for you. But Eric, this might be farewell, but it's not goodbye. I don't know about heaven, but I do know a bit about atoms (thanks, Mr Malhotra from Year 5), and so I know that no one ever really disappears. They just kind of change form. And, if you think about it, Eric, that means that one day, maybe not tomorrow, and maybe not even a thousand years from now, but one day our atoms will make two new things, maybe two new people, I don't know, but it sounds cool, and I hope it happens, and I hope, one day, I get to meet you again.

Over and out, Eric Griffin. Over and out.

"Roger that, Finn Jones," I muttered, wiping my eyes with my hands. "Roger that."

Cooper reached over and squeezed my hand. "You OK?"

I nodded. "I'm OK." I cleared my throat and blinked a bunch of times, then opened the bag of chips I'd got for Finn. "I don't know why I'm doing this, it just feels right," I said.

"You don't need a reason," Cooper replied. "If it feels right, then it is right."

I turned to Cooper and smiled. "You're a good friend, Cooper. I'm sorry if I haven't been such a good one to you, but I'm going to try. If you'll let me?"

Coops grinned, squeezing my shoulder. "Mates. Definitely."

I smiled, then spread the unwrapped packet out on the wall next to me, sad that Finn wasn't there to enjoy the chips with me, but taking comfort that, somehow, he was still there for me, he always would be, and the things he'd taught me, the laughs we'd had, the good times we'd shared, they would always be ours, and Finn would live on; in them, in the memory, in my stories, and in me.

And just as I was smiling about that, a massive great seagull swooped down, landed next to Finn's chips, and gobbled up a beakful. Then it looked at me, chips hanging out of its beak, cocked its head, and, I swear, it winked at me.

And then, in a flap of wings, it flew away into the sky and disappeared over the horizon.

I laughed. And Cooper laughed.

"ENJOY YOUR CHIPS, FINN JONES!" I shouted.

We laughed some more, and we ate chips, and we soaked up the last of the warm evening sun, and although it didn't feel quite right still, it felt a little bit better.

"Go on then," Cooper said, as he finished his final chip. "Tell me a Finn story. Tell me how you first met."

So I did.

CHAPTER TWENTY-EIGHT

6 years ago

I must have been about six years old – I was in Year 2 anyway. Somehow, I already had a reputation as this pathetic, cowardly kid who no one really wanted to spend time with. I used to hang out by myself at break time. Tragic, really.

Then, one day, this new kid arrived. And his name was Finn Jones. He was so confident, and so happy, and so funny, and I wished I could be like him. It was like he just … threw himself into life, with so much enjoyment. For some reason, and I won't ever understand why, Finn started talking to me one break time and he suggested we go down the big slide in the play area. Massive thing, it was – I mean, it wouldn't seem massive now, but back then, it felt super dangerous, and Mum had warned me so often about doing dangerous things. I told him how scared I was, and he said it would be fine and told me the plan: he'd go down first, and then once I'd seen it wasn't dangerous, I should follow.

I liked that. There was a plan.

"OK?" Finn said. "Over and out!"

"What does that mean?" I asked.

"It's what two soldiers say to each other when they have a plan. One says 'Over and out!' and the other says 'Roger that!' to show they understand."

I nodded. "Roger that!"

"Exactly!" Finn beamed.

Finn clambered up the steps to the top of the slide, talking to me as I followed behind, telling me it was all gonna be fine.

He sat down at the top, shouted, "Over and Out!" and *whoosh!* shot off down the slide.

"Come on!" he shouted up from the bottom. "You've gotta do it, else how will you get back down anyway?"

He had a point.

So I sat at the top, shaking because of the height, then looked at Finn, smiling at me, eyes sparkling, looking so kind and so lovely, and all I wanted in that moment was to be standing next to Finn again, because he was the first person who had ever been nice to me. And even though I was scared, I did it. I shot down the slide. Because with Finn, suddenly the world seemed a less scary place.

"Yay!" Finn said, high-fiving me when I reached the bottom.

I was giggling with the adrenaline.

Finn gave me a hug. "You and me, we're gonna be best friends. OK? You and me, Eric, we're gonna take on the whole world and we're gonna win! Everyone will know our names! Best mates. Forever! Over and out!"

I laughed. "Roger that, Finn Jones. Roger that!"

ACKNOWLEDGEMENTS

Thank you to: Linas Alsenas, Sarah Dutton, Tierney Holm, Sarah Baldwin, Susila Baybars, Harriet Dunlea, Hannah Griffiths, Ellen Thomson, Catherine Bell, Antonia Pelari, the brilliant team at Scholastic UK, everyone at Bounce, Jo Moult at Skylark Literary, Sarah Counsell, The Cavs, and all my friends and family.

A special shout out to Jennifer Jamieson who drew all the beautiful illustrations for the book – aren't they fabulous?! I love them very much and I think Finn would approve too.

A big thank you to all the teachers and librarians who continue to champion my books in their schools and libraries. And a very big thank you to all the bookshops, booksellers, bloggers and reviewers who have supported *Finn Jones*.

Thank you to Child Bereavement UK for reading a draft of *Finn Jones* and being so very kind about it – I really appreciate and value your feedback.

This book is dedicated to my dad, who never got to see any of my books published, or, indeed, get to see his own name on one of his own books – so here it is, Dad, next best thing.

Thanks to all of you for reading. I hope you enjoyed it, and if any of you are going through similar things to Eric, then I hope it helped a bit.

And, of course, to Eric Griffin and Finn Jones – thank you for trusting me with your story. I hope I did it justice.

Over and out!

Simon

Photo: YellowBelly

SIMON JAMES GREEN

Simon James Green is an award-winning author of books for children and young adults. He has been shortlisted for the YA Book Prize, the Diverse Book Awards, the Lollies, has won the Bristol Teen Book Award and been twice nominated for the Carnegie medal. His first middle-grade novel, *Life of Riley: Beginner's Luck*, was shortlisted for the Blue Peter Book Award and won the Fantastic Book Awards 2022. *Sleepover Takeover* was shortlisted for the Oxfordshire Book Awards 2023 and featured in the Great Book's Guide from BookTrust. He has also written two picture books, illustrated by Garry Parsons: *Llama Glamarama* and *Fabulous Frankie*. He lives in London and loves puzzles and escape rooms as much as Finn and Eric.

For more information on Simon visit:

www.simonjamesgreen.com

JENNIFER JAMIESON

Jennifer is an illustrator living in the sunny English countryside. She loves creating quirky, feisty and friendly characters and bringing their wonderful personalities to life. When Jennifer isn't drawing bemused cats for children's books, she likes to draw bemused cats for fun. Because drawing is so much fun even when it's your job! She loves the idea that we can change the world by the books we read, and believes every message is best delivered with a bit of humour.

You can find out more about Jennifer at:
www.jenniferjamieson.com
or follow her on Instagram
@jen_jamieson

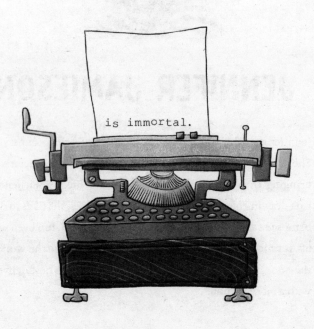

is immortal.